First Printing, June 15, 2025

ISBN : 979-8-9920290-3-1

This book is dedicated to my late father Peter, my
mother Leticia, my wife Cheri, my children Prince,
Malaika and Cameron. Also, to my family friends and
close supporters. Thank you.
"We Give God the Glory."

UBOA ACT 2

UBOA ACT 2

Prince Otchere

Contents

1

The Hurt Manifested

Deep within the abysmal wilderness amongst the uncharted forest, Adam was found pacing alone. He clung arrogantly to the triumphant feeling of righteousness and superiority which helped to nurse his bruised ego. Adam reflected on his brazen actions with defiance and mixed emotions. The experience he believed would serve as a potent message to the others reminding them of man's plight and destined path to greatness. These highly complex and complicated feelings only help to inflate and further Adams sense of ego and righteousness. He swaggered about gracefully with a posturing strut and somewhat noticeable dip and in his stride. Adam appeared determined if not committed more than ever to uncovering the origin and source of the strange noise. He amused himself with celebratory thoughts of returning to the garden with the noise maker victoriously secured in hand. Adam ventured onward in his path carrying the unshakable conviction and belief that the strange noise was nothing more than a lost or wounded creature. He assumed the strange noise was the cry of a helpless animal having somehow lost their way. Adam imagined that one of the inhabitants had stumbled into the outskirts and was now stranded and lost confined within its trenches. The reasonable assumptions Adam produced were at times challenged by his overactive imagination which conjured frightening and unsavory images and helpless creature.

These thoughts and more occupied Adam's mind and helped to make the long journey tolerable. Adam did not appear nervous but instead drew excitement at the potential possibilities conjured in his mind. He was optimistic and held firm to the notion of possibilities that occupied his private thoughts. Adam imagined the looks of astonishment plastered across the faces of the very cynics who had initially mocked and doubted him. He postured slightly with a defiant grin appearing very much settled by the conclusion and outcome of his vivid imagination. He relished the thought of seeing the looks on the faces of the creatures after unveiling the source of their distress. Adam was determined to successfully bring a climatic end to the mysterious noise maker driving the garden into fearful panic and uproar. "I must find it." Adam announced with growing determination. He aimed to draw looks of agony and defeat from the smug faces of the many doubters and naysayers. "That would make this journey truly worthwhile." Adam snickered to himself. He managed to stay positive finding amusement in his current moment of strife. Humor helped to distract Adam from the turmoil of his raging thoughts which at the times appeared embittered and filled with anguish.

It was nearly dawn when Adam arrived at the edge of Eden in full view of the grand wall. He slowed his pace and began to tread cautiously taking special notice of the dimming glow of the evening sky. The patchy pathway leading to the grand wall was hard and rough. The coursed trail was filled with debris and fragments of small stones and rocks. The massive figure of the grand wall was protected and fenced off by a preceding layer of unwanted plants and noxious weeds. The barrier of invasive plants appeared elongated and protruded upward like scaling stems and vegetation. The giant fern would be Adams first obstacle in his path and journey to the grand wall. Adam stood poised in silence watching what he observed as a field of tall grass receding before the bordering walls. Left with no formal path thru the grassy terrain, Adam resorted to carve his own path stepping forcefully into the grassy field. Adam attempted to penetrate the dense layer of thicket however he was met with resistance.

Adam struggled to move his body thru the dense bushes forcefully pushing forward with every step. He found it difficult to maneuver and navigate through the thick barrier of herbage. At times Adam found himself lost at times within the mossy labyrinth. He used brute force and strength to force his way through the thick layer of fern and brushwood. He ignored the stinging pain from the sprigs of thorned stems scraping and cutting against the softness of his body and skin. Overcome with exhaustion and fatigue Adam became somewhat numbed to the pain. He could no longer feel his body after receiving several injuries caused by the grassy thicket of sharp blades. Adam appeared rather unprepared and outmatched against the abusive terrain beating violently against his body. He was determined to meet his goal by overcoming all obstacles that stood in his way. Fueled by adrenaline and somewhat of an inflated ego he was persistent in furthering his goal and pushing on against the might and strength of the scaling meadow. Adam persevered through the large field combing past the few stems and bristles that remained before emerging triumphantly on the other end.

Adam now found himself standing only meters away from the massive grand wall. The sight of the monumental structure stood as a marvelous enigma to be admired. The grand wall scaled high, and was vast in length, the gigantic structure was enormous peaking upwards of sixty to one hundred feet. No creature had ever stood as close to the grand wall as Adam was standing now. He grazed his hands delicately over the large structure showing great admiration to the raw texture and integrity of the massive stones. Adam was drawn and oddly captivated by the grand wall before him. The molding of stone and cinder was no easy feat thought Adam looking on with astonishment at the marveling monument. The wall stood as a testimonial to the power and capabilities of its architect. Adam imagined the creator was an incredibly powerful being ginormous in build and structure harnessing unbelievable strength and power.

Adam stood before the grand wall totally engrossed with fascination consumed by the colorful ideas that filled his imagination. Suddenly a strange noise interrupted the silent dead air of the night. The unfamiliar sound did not startle or frighten Adam, but instead it seized and gripped his attention. The noise seemed strangely familiar, and listening closely, he tried desperately to discern the faint sound. "The strange noise," thought Adam, "resembling that of whimpering outcry being carried beneath the echoing wind."

Adam's curiosity and eagerness sought to uncover the direction of the strange sounds. He propelled his feet giving chase to the fleeting outcry and following his ears he moved quickly in direction of the of strange sound. Adam was painfully reminded of the rocky terrain beneath his feet and adjusted quickly by moving delicately over the piles of scattered stones and jagged rocks surrounding the base of the grand wall. The sharp stones and jagged rocks served as a tertiary defense and deterrent against uninvited intruders. However, Adam was relentless in his pursuit of vindication. He was determined more than ever to fulfill his objective of uncovering the source and origin of the strange noise.

Adam walked on the dusty ground stepping carefully as to avoid accidental harm, and injury. The soles of his feet were unfamiliar to strange terrain and began to ache and grow sore. Adam dismissed the pain continuing his path and pursuit of the strange noise. The strange sound was unbearably irritating and unpleasant but eerily familiar. The sound carried a tone and pitch that was unrecognizable to most creatures, however Adam being naturally intuitive was able to decipher the strange sound as a cry for help. An overwhelming sense of sadness and empathy began to consume Adam as he struggled to listen to the painful outcries echoing in the air. The sound of helplessness evoked distant memories within Adam. He began to recall instances where he himself had succumb to the pitfalls and foxholes of life. He empathized with the strange noise by remembering his own shortcomings as a child. The pleading cries for support many of which went unmet. The sentimental and somewhat emotional thought became the premise and reason for which Adam would use to justify and further his cause.

Adam began to slow his pace as he approached a large fracture in the wall. He was convinced that the strange eerie noise was a call for help. The large dent and burrowed scar appeared unnatural, like a disfiguring hole deliberately etched into the side of the grand wall defacing the monument. The break in the wall was rather minor and considerably small in proportion to enormous scale of the giant wall. The fracture was hardly noticeable when standing off in the distance, then in proximity. Standing up-close Adam felt compelled to examine the gaping hole. He found himself strangely drawn to the trenches of the grand wall. Adam inspected the obscurely large dent up close. "Some sort of damage was done here." He assessed quickly looking over the jagged area. He peered directly into the dark hole examining the radius and depth of the narrow entry.

Adam discovered a shadowy figure lodged within the slated jaws of the lofty rocks. The helpless creature appeared trapped within the confines of walls womb. Adam rejoiced with excitement at uncovering the source of the strange noise. Overly ambitious and eager to claim his reward he proceeded to plunge his arms into the dark abysmal hole. However, the risky attempt deemed futile as Adam was unable to reach the confined creature. He attempted with desperation to squeeze his body through the narrow break but was unable to get his rigid body through the narrow opening. "Had, I been smaller, and more agile" Adam thought, "I could easily have maneuvered through this hole." Adam placed his face up against the wide opening of the wall hoping to catch a better glimpse of the ensnared creature, however the absence of light provided him no way of fully viewing the creature

The frightened creature which had been wailing and whimpering stopped suddenly after being startled by Adam's sudden appearance. The creature began to panic, breathing nervously consumed by terror at the thought of impeding danger. The creature produced a wave of alarming outcries which were piercingly loud and sharp. The loud noises were quickly becoming an unpleasant sound that served as a deterrent for Adam. He was beginning to reconsider his attempt to rescue the detained creature. The excessive sound of whimpering felt terribly unsettling to the point that Adam could scarcely withstand the sound. He grappled with his nerves feeling somewhat put off and discouraged by the strange sounds however Adam refused to turn away or submit.

"Do not be afraid" Adam assured yelling directly into the crevasse and ear of the large opening. The sound of his voice startled the trapped creature once again to the point the creature gave out a shrieking outcry. The shadowy figure cried out fearfully and began to squirm and juke hysterically. The determined creature struggled tirelessly to free itself from the gripping clutches of the confined space. The creature squirmed and tugged, shifted and twisted until finally a hard tug managed to help free one of its limbs. The moment of freedom was short lived as the creature worked to free another limb and body part. The creature juked and jolted rocking back forth in an effort build momentum before lunging forward headfirst. The preemptive misstep would cost the creature severely after hitting its head against the roof of the inner wall. The blunt impact of the collision ultimately caused the creature to fall into a state of unconsciousness.

The loud thump unnerved and startled Adam forcing him to jump back and clutch tightly to his pounding chest. Adam was engulfed in fear his nerves shook frantically growing rather apprehensive and uncertain of untamed creature lodged in between the corroded rocks. Adam struggled to regain his composure and breath he panted desperately in attempt to sooth and regain his quivering nerves. Adam slid down to ground with his back against the wall. He was consumed with fear and terror very much so that he began revisit the overall objective and purpose of his mission. Adam sat with the personal and somewhat moral dilemma of whether he should continue his futile attempt to aid the helpless creature. Or make his untimely exit and retreat to the garden where he would offer a full report of his findings to Tree, and the others.

The thought of returning empty handed and having to explain his shortcomings to the pompous inhabitants of the garden instantly filled Adam with rage. He recalled the abuse and mistreatment that he received and began to grow rather angry. Their cruel treatment and behavior towards appeared inadmissible and deserved an equally appropriate response of ridicule and humiliation. In managing his unsettled nerves Adam began to slowly regain his composure. He grappled somewhat with the prickling emotions of fear and anger dueling inside of him.

Some serious consideration was given by Adam on whether to continue with this maddening task. His decision on the matter waw observed as he began slowly to peer his head back up to face the dark hole. Adam drew his eyes towards the large crevice with the hopes of distinguishing creature trapped between the walls. The dark hole unlit and scarce of light made it difficult for Adam to place eyes on the shadowy creature coiled beneath the smothering rocks. "But how did the creature become so entrapped?" Adam contemplated while considering ways in which to proceed safely. Adam wanted very much to help the poor creature, however not at the expense of causing damage or potential injury to himself.

Adam soon recovered his nerves and moving rather hastily he managed to raise himself back onto his feet. He hurled his upper body into the dark hole while still having his legs and lower body firmly planted at the base of the grand wall. Adam struggled a great deal stretching himself painfully thin to fit the dark narrow hole. He extended the tips of his toes to help elevate and extend his reach into the large gaping hole. "Hello, please do not be startled!" Adam called out in a precarious attempt to sooth the savage creature and discourage the possibility of another outcry. Adam was unaware that the creature was presently in a motionless state and took the silent response as an act of acknowledgment and consent. "Please, do not cry out," Adam pleaded, "If you allow it, I believe that I may be of assistance to you." The creature responded with stoic silence which Adam once again interpreted as an informal reception to his services. "I am here to help you."

Adam attempted to stretch his body beyond the boundaries of its limits. He forced the frame of his body deep into the abysmal hole clawing away frantically in desperation. Adam garnered what little strength remained extending his lanky arms to further his range and reach of the helpless creature. "Grab hold of me" Adam yelled out, but the creature did not move or stir. Adam slammed his body against the wall attempting frantically to reach further into deep hole. He struggled to maneuver and squeeze his limbs into tight opening. Adam pushed and tugged jerking his upper body into the narrow entry of hole. Warm beads of sweat began to form over Adams face and body like moist dew. The exhaustive lubricant which marinated his body was purposeful in allowing Adam to squirm further into the hole gaining a few extra inches of reaching space.

Adam reached out in hopes of grabbing hold of the creatures' arms or limbs, but all he could feel was the creatures lengthy fur grazing and brushing against his forearm. Adam managed to clasp onto the creature and began a desperate effort to free the trapped creature from the tight grip and clutches of the grand wall. Adam worked tirelessly as the beads of sweat now began to pool and form beneath his drenching body. Water seemed to pour and drip down from every part of his body. Adam managed successfully to secure a firm hold on the creature by clamping his arms around one of the creature's limbs. He was now relying on the strength of his back and lower body to heave and pull him out narrow opening. Adam mustered all the strength of his lower half to pull him as well as the creature from the trenches of the wall. Adam inched further back out with every heave and forceful tug. He shifted the weight of his body back and forth. He intended to thrust and pull the creature from the hole, but a minor misstep caused Adam's body to collide against the rough jagged edges. "Ahhh!" Adam cried out painfully "My side. It pains me! Unfortunately for Adam there was no time for him to nurse the excruciating pain felt from experiencing a fractured and possibly broken a rib. He struggled with the pain until finally a fierce jolt and forceful thrust released them from the confining hold of the grand wall.

Adam was able to free the creature, but somehow managed to injure himself in the process. The heaving struggle sent Adam stumbling backwards losing hold on the creature as well as his footing. He tumbled backwards and fell hard against the ground. Adam found himself on his back tired and drained, somewhat disoriented. He struggled to get back up but discovered that he was much too weak and overcome with exhaustion. On his back Adam laid smiling, looking up laughing at the twinkling stars, he watched as the glimmering sky churned slowly around him. He turned his head to the side to look over at creature he had struggled to rescue stretched out alongside him. The creature having been afflicted with head injury was at present still unconscious. Adam struggled to get a good look at the creature however could not clearly make out a clear image due to what appeared to be long strains of mane and fur draped over the creature's face.

Smiling up at the moon Adam began to laugh hysterically recounting the act of bravery and heroism. There was no doubt that Adam was delightfully pleased by the conquest of his daring rescue. He relished over the victorious moment with immeasurable pride. Adam replayed over in his mind an exaggerated and somewhat cinematic rendition of the events that just took place. The familiar weariness of the night ushered in a sense of calm of serenity over the land. Adam's chest rose and fell with every breath drawn from his flaring nostrils. His watery eyes were very much fixed on the glittering starriness of the twinkling night. The burden of Adams's weary eyelids would eventually collapse beneath the weight of exhaustion. The restful act would help send Adam into a much-needed state of peacefully sleep and rest.

2

The Meet

Adam awoke with the rising of the sun to find himself alone near the pasture. The creature that he helped to rescue was nowhere to be found. It appeared the creature had awoken before Adam and fled off following the trailed path made by him. He found himself somewhat annoyed by the creature's hasty departure without properly thanking him. Adam slowly rose to his feet, and immediately clutched his side still very much sore. He took immediate notice to the speckle of reddish blots which stained the ground leading back into the patchy plain. Adam followed the pitter-patter of strange substance and liquid he would later discover as blood. "The" liquid matter Tree summarized in her reference to biology "was contained within all living creatures and organisms." Adam followed the scarlet trail back and very soon found himself back in the mossy fertile lands of Eden. He walked toward the path and direction of the riverbank.

The riverbank was the declared the quenching grounds where all the creatures in the garden gathered and communed regularly. It was there that Adam found the creature that he helped to rescue swimming carelessly in the shallow banks of the clear water. The creature swam effortlessly with a familiar sense of ease and grace that Adam nearly mistook the creature for a large aquatic fish or sea urchin of some sorts.

After watching for some time Adam began to question and wonder if the creature, he rescued was indeed a water dweller or some-

11

thing more. This thought only help to peak Adam's curiosity and heighten his interest to pursue and engage the creature. Adam silently crept around the outskirts of the pond, before moving in closer in hopes of gaining a better view. He managed to remain concealed hiding himself near the edge of the pond behind a thicket of wild bushes. Adam had secured the perfect angle, the perfect view and vantage point that would allow him to better study and understand the strange creature. It did not take very long for Adam to succumb to the creatures mesmerizing beauty. He confessed openly to never having witnessed or laid eyes on such a wonderful and enchanting being.

Adam appeared infatuated by the creature before him and began slowly drawing out from behind the shadows. Eager and overly anxious, Adam was prepared to disregard the subtleties of formal introduction and initiate his very own meet cute. He stood up from the leering shadows stepping out from behind the veil of shrubbery into the light. Adam's intention and was to avoid being spotted by the strange creature.

The creature was unaware of Adam lurking in the background and appeared more preoccupied with washing away traces of blood that soaked and stained the creature's lengthy mane and scalp. The creature awoke before Adam in a state of panic and confusion. The creature struggled to recall any fond or distant memories which would help to provide context or explain the present situation. As it appeared the forgetful creature could not remember much of anything since waking from the brief coma like state. The creature surveyed the area searching desperately for a familiar landmark or relic of some sorts. However unfortunate the creature was unable to bare any recollection of the unfamiliar landscape. Feeling utterly lost and confused the creature began to experience a sense of displacement The latent inability to access memories was partially due to traumatic brain injury. The impactful blow caused what appeared to be a concussion as result of the heralding escape. The creature somehow managed to nurse its wounds, attending to the small gash on its head with a mixture of moist earth and leafy minerals. Silently leering from across the water like a predator studying its prey was Adam. He watched with growing intrigue and fascination at the unsuspecting creature tending its wounds. The vantage point which Adam presently occupied provided him a clear view of the creature, and at the same time minimized the risk and chance of being exposed or uncovered.

Adam exercised agility to shorten the distance between him and the creature. He moved stealthily taking refuge in the shadowy backdrop behind a veil of shrubbery and thin blades of long grass. He was now in proximity of the creature standing only meters away in distance. Adam could see the creature's full design, observing clearly the naked and moistened body of the strange visitor. Adam was very much surprised to discover that the creatures frame and design was no different from that of his own. The unfamiliar creature was a remarkable specimen drawing much of Adams captivation and interest. It would not take Adam very long before finding himself becoming enchanted by the loveliness and mystique of the strange visitor. Adam was dumbfounded and stricken somewhat taken aback by the creature's curvaceous allure and appealing qualities. These attributes seemed to heighten Adams curiosity and attraction to the strange creature. Adam was now daunted with the overwhelming impulse and task to approach and engage the creature.

Adam appeared delightfully surprised as he was expecting to find a hairy four-legged beast. The hideous image he conjured from their initial encounter lodged together in the shadowy wall. Adam managed to evade being sighted by staying away from the creature's peripheral view. Adam drew closer to the creature and attempted to reach out and touch the creature to offer a meaningful greeting and introduction. However, the startled creature reacted instinctively to the shock and surprise of Adam's touch and screamed out in fear. The terrified creature shrieked louder and began to splash water as a repellent to keep Adam away. The freighted creature spun around quickly in a desperate attempt to flee. The quick motion and sudden turnabout served as a useful deterrent in keeping Adam at bay. He received a moist slap across the face from the creatures long-wet mane. The sudden splash surprised Adam who reacted instinctively by quickly pulling back his hand. Adam appeared frozen with confusion his face and body entirely drenched and soaked in water. Despite the demonstration Adam remained steadfast refusing to allow the inglorious moment to dampen his mood or shift his focus from engaging the creature. He kept his eyes fixed on the creature who by this time was fearfully retreating, Adam was still baffled and yet still fascinated by the artistry and design of the strange being.

Adam studied the creature closely and began to consider the idea and notion that he and the creature were of similar quality and pedigree. "The stranger has arms and legs and moves like I do." Adam thought to himself, however not entirely convinced. Adam looked on at the creature with bewildering confusion somewhat puzzled by the exaggeration of body parts mounted on the creature. Adam regarded the creature as a being of his own likeness, although the creature displayed some observable distinctions and differences. Adam was thrilled at the idea of meeting another creature like himself. He thought about the restless nights and lonely days he endured longing for the company of another. He recalled with bitterness the daunting feeling of loneliness that taunted him regularly. The celebratory title of rare and unique would eventually serve as thorning reminder foreshadowing a life of solitude and loneliness. "This is amazing," Adam rejoiced, "I was told that there existed no other creature like me in Eden, but today I am fortunate to have encountered another rare and enchanting creature. The sublime creature and I appear nearly identical in makeup and design." Adam's growing fascination for the creature caused him to exercise poor judgment. Throwing concern, and caution to the wind Adam willfully accepted the new creature as flawlessly crafted and wonderfully made. "It is undeniably obvious to see," Adam retorted to himself "that both the creature and I were both designed by the same masterful hands."

There were three distinctive disfigurements, which quickly caught Adams attention. He pondered on the state of the architect that molded such a puzzling creature. There were certain exaggerations in the creatures' attributes and design which puzzled Adam. The first noticeable flaw observed by Adam was that the creature owned an outrageous amount of fur on its head. The mane like substance draped like dark linen down the creature's back and chest.

The creature's hair was observably much lengthier than that of his own. Adam pondered for some time searching his mind for a reasonable purpose or value for such lengthy hair. Though Adam attempted to come up with a reason, he was unable comprehend or decipher the intended purpose and benefits of owning such excessive amount of hair. Adam considered the plausible possibility that the long hair was a utility of some sorts used to help regulate and sustain internal temperature. "Yes, that must be it." Adam deduced with confidence fully committed to the reasonable notion and belief that the creature's mane served as a provisional coverlet which helped to support the creature's vagrant and somewhat transient lifestyle. The bountiful hair assured the unhoused creature's survival by providing additional barrier of protection against the unforeseen elements.

Adam concluded the matter accepting his notion and theory as empirical truth. It was during this scrutinous examination that Adam admittedly began to admire the creatures flowing hair and began viewing the lengthy mane subjectively as being rather unique and distinguishable trait. In a slow and subtle embrace Adam began to slowly withdraw his original opinion quickly redacting the initial complaint in viewing the creature's luxurious mane as flawed. Adam now saw the extensive growth as being a rather distinctive and alluring trait that only help to further enhance the creature's physical appearance.

The second observable flaw Adam highlighted was the strange oddity in the creature's body and framework. He took notice of the creature's shape and design appearing somewhat puzzled by its disproportionate build and size. The slender creature appeared disfigured and unportioned. "The creatures small frame contradicts that of its protruding upper body." Adam observed, he studied the creature closely riddled with enigma at the pair of fat glands mounted across the creature's chest. "A strangely peculiar location to place barons." Adam thought to himself viewing the unfamiliar body part as hefty anchors or weights of some sorts. He deduced with childish reasoning that the two large bosoms served to keep the delicate creature vertically grounded. Still very much young and impressionable Adam saw the bearings as supplemental weights. They served to minimize the risk and likelihood of being carried away by the forceful winds.

Adam questioned the legitimacy of his theory and hypothesis as unsubstantiated. He patiently studied the creatures' anatomy with the hope of finding a physiological trait that would reveal some indication as to the creature's history and origin. He reserved a private thought believing that the creature had somehow managed to break free and escape a life of indentured servitude. Adam was overcome with sympathy and compassion for the isolated creature, he empathized with the creatures identifying fully with the creature's plight and unfair treatment. "Are you alright?" Adam asked with genuine concern and attempted to reach out and touch the creature again. The nervous creature refused to be handled and shrieked loudly before plunging into the water. Submerged beneath the clear water the creature ascended periodically for air with the lingering hope that Adam would leave or go away.

Adam observed the creature's evasive behavior with tactful lenses and attributed the creature's prolonged submersion was partly related to its robust glands. He reconsidered his previous notion adopting a new theory and idea about the strange creature. Adam entertained the thought that somehow the creatures' protruding chest housed an extra set of lungs contained outside its body. He imagined that the fatty tissue somehow stored additional air making it possible for the creature to remain submerged for longer periods. "Amazing," Adam thought, "simply remarkable." The concept seemed probable however faired unpractical as Adam would soon come to learn. He stood patiently by the of the river waiting for the creature to emerge. He was prepared to wait assuming the busty sacks would allow the creature to remain beneath the water for a substantial amount of time. However, after a few brief seconds the creature emerged from the depths of the water panting and splashing about desperate for air. The creature greedily inhaled taking in as much oxygen and air into its lungs and bosoms as it possibly could.

The third and final flaw observed by Adam was that the creature was absent or rather missing its lower appendage. Adam gave the idea much thought but could not conceive a possible explanation as to why the creature did not have or own a lower organ. Adam used his logical reasoning but could not conceive any plausible or significant benefits to not retaining such an important and vital body part. "How does the creature relieve itself?" Adam pondered gazing curiously with his eyes fixed on the creature. He watched as the creature paddled away swimming away franticly in the opposite direction towards the shallow end of the river. The creature splashed and kicking repeatedly in the water attempting to flee, oblivious and unaware of Adam pacing alongside the large bed of land surrounding the water. Adam resembled a forceful and relentless predator, scouring over an elusive and cunning prey. The creature retained a natural affinity and prowess that seemed to reinforce Adams attraction and growing feelings for the strange being. Despite demonstrating a brooding lack of interest, the creatures had accidently lured and snagged the affection and fascination of a specific prince.

It was apparent that Adam fancied the new creature watching on with adoration as the flighty creature attempted to secure a means of escape. Adam did not understand how such a creature could produce within him such a heightened sense of joy and euphoria. He experienced for the first time illicit emotions and warm feelings that were unfamiliar and foreign to him. He carried intimate thoughts while in a love induced daydream. He fantasized having befriended the creature and becoming likely companions. These thoughts and more easily led Adam to stumble face first into the uncharted territory of seduction and romance. The creature on the other hand did not share Adams' sentiments or understand the reason for his persistent act and pursuit. The creature very much fearful for its life swam desperately in attempt to evade the unknown and relentless pursuer. The nimble creature swam with a sense of urgency moving quickly through the tepid waters. The rhythm of swift motions demonstrated a sense of urgency as the creature reacted instinctively by initiating its fight or flight response. The creature was now halfway across the river rapidly approaching the other end of the shore. Despite struggling with exhaustion, the creature paddled and stroked tirelessly to reach the other end of the river.

It was no secret that Adam was a novice to the complex rituals and dynamics of courtship. He had never experienced attraction towards another creature before this very moment. Adam held the firm belief that the mysterious creature was not an identical replica as previously suggested. He now saw the creature through a visually stunning lens adorned with boundless beauty. Adam's judgement appeared clouded by new feelings and emotions unfolding deep within him. The sudden emergence of these foreign emotions appeared difficult for Adam to navigate and process. He was still unsure exactly how to describe or explain his attraction and fascination with the creature. It went without saying the creature's beauty and mystique helped to justify the warrant and pursuit of Adams attraction.

Adam found it difficult to commit to an exact reasoning for his interest. He lengthened his stride, racing quickly to meet the creature edging closer to the land. Adam felt a sense of shame and embarrassment reflecting on his earlier attempt to initiate an introduction. He felt somewhat compelled to offer an apology with the hopes of amending the prior incident which had just taken place

Adam arrived just time to meet the creature drawing closer to the shore. The creature appeared exhausted crawling on all fours while gasping desperately for air. Adam began to rescind his original assumption initially labeling the strange creature as partly aquatic and preferring water over land. "Let me help you." Adam offered his assistance extending his arms waiting patiently for the creature to accept his hand. Unsure exactly how to respond, the weary creature began to slowly withdraw inching closer to the water. Adam observed the creature's hesitation and apprehension and quickly retracted his hand hopping the gesture would someway alleviate any misgivings or tension.

Adam did not want to startle the timid creature or cause it to flee back into the murky water. In gesturing his surrender Adam placed his arms in the air to expose his inner palms. "Alright," assured Adam, stepping back allowing for distance and space between them both. "Do not be afraid." Assured Adam offering a friendly smile that help to reassure the frightened and confused creature gazing awkwardly. Adam seemed more confident and poised communicating with nervous and somewhat apprehensive creature. He no longer nursed emotions of fear and uncertainty speaking tenderly to the nervous and confused being.

Adam was now standing before the creature attempting to provoke discourse and dialogue through engagement. "Do not be afraid," Adam restated once again, attempting to reassure to creature. "My name is Adam, and I live here in Eden. What is your name?" The creature listened carefully to Adam without providing him an answer or response. The creature remained silent wearing a look skepticism masked with terror and confusion. "Where do you come from?" Adam questioned the creature with the hopes of prompting an answer from the seemingly unresponsive creature.

"When I first discovered you" Adam reminded the creature "you were trapped burrowed deep within in the grand wall." The creature attempted to recall the incident described but found it difficult to remember much of anything. "I helped to rescue you," Adam explained stepping forward slowly, "I saved you by pulling you from in between the grips of the large rocks." The creature began to grow nervous observing Adam drawing closer however the creature did not retreat or flee into the water.

This is Eden" Adam announced pointing around at the beautiful landscape surrounding them. "Eden is my home, where are you from?" The creature glanced back at the pond as if in pre-contemplation of a plan or means to escape. Adam could tell that the creature was still uneasy, and nervous by their encounter. "You do not have to jump back in," Adam suggested stepping aside to provide a path of egress for the creature to exit freely. The creature seemed to grow more skeptical viewing the gesture as being a possible ruse or trick.

The creature stepped back carefully moving delicately into the direction of the river's edge. And without offering a sign or warning the creature suddenly sprang forth dashing quickly past Adam. The narrow escape was brief and short lived as the creature tumbled suddenly on to the ground. The slippery terrain of moist mud caused the creature to accidently lose its footing and fall. Filled with humiliation and embarrassment the creature attempted to raise itself from the muddied floor but accidentally stumbled a few more times. The hilarious spectacle caused Adam some much needed amusement finding it difficult to control his laugher. The creature sat pitifully on the ground covered entirely with dirt and mud. The creature seemed annoyed and upset by the sound of Adams laughter but ignored the noise, concerned more so with the prospect of standing up while avoiding the ground.

Adam appeared suddenly hovering over the creature. His shadow cast a dark figure over the creature that seemed to paralyze the frozen creature unable to look up at him. Adam did not speak or utter a sound, but instead knelt before the creature to once again offer his hand. The kind gesture was not immediately received however Adam demonstrated patience in his offer to help the fallen creature up from the ground. The moment began to draw more awkward with the flushed creature leering nervously over the set of open hands offering support. The muddied creature looked around in search of an outlet or means to get away, but unfortunately there was no means of escape.

The creature quietly submitted and began slowly to extend and reach out to meet Adams hand. He gripped the creature's hand and proceeded to pull the creature up from its present lowly state. He helped the creature back to its feet, while gently removing traces of mud and debris smeared on the creature's face. Adam helped to guide the creature back into water to help cleanse away the remaining mud. He did the best that he could to wash away and remove the stain of clay off the creature's body before stepping back out into the open air.

Adam happily assisted to the creature with getting out of the water, he offered a gentle tug which sent the creature flying into his arms. Adam grasped the creature firmly in his arms as their eyes met for first time. The two shared a long and intimate gaze which last briefly however felt much longer. Adam could feel the warmth of the creature's skin pulsating against his body. He embraced the creature with a reassuring smile which to seemed to demonstrate the nature of his goodwill and intentions. Adam had never experienced this level of joy and ecstasy in the presence of another creature. His sentiments mirrored that of the grand wall both in stature and possessiveness. Adam clung firmly to the creature body as though refusing to let go.

Adam's thoughts roamed aimlessly guided only by the swelling emotions that fluttered deep within his body. The two creatures moved their bodies rhythmically as if dancing to the thumping rhythm of their beating hearts. Entangled in Adams arms was a creature of immaculate beauty, and artistry. Adam peered deeply into the creature's eyes and was overcome with an unshakable sense of gratitude and favor. He no longer seemed concerned with uncovering the trivial details of the creature's history and origin. He was choosing instead to prioritize the sensation of joy and excitement that he was presently experiencing at having discovered a creature identical to himself.

Adam being consumed and engrossed in his thoughts was scarcely unaware of the strange freakishly large grin that he now bore. The creature looked at Adam rather puzzled not fully comprehending the reason for his suspense and delight. Adam's large smile somewhat perverse in angle resembled that of a mischievous grin. "You are safe with me," He reassured, the creature however the creature did not answer or speak but responded suddenly by passing out in his arms. The creatures sudden swooning drew concern regarding the health and state of the frail creature. Adam questioned whether his tight hold on the creature had caused the creature to faint. Adam assessed the creature like a physician before quickly ruling out his hand in the matter. The untrained medic though minimally skilled managed to gather and rule out the creature's symptoms. Adam deduced that the creature had simply exerted too much energy and was presently experiencing the exhaustive repercussions. Ignoring the intense discomfort and pain in his side Adam managed to lift the creature beyond the threshold of the water bank. He shifted the creature from his arms onto his shoulders to alleviate the discomfort. Adam began his journey home to the garden carrying the noise maker back with him.

Adam tread the back into the jungle and scoured aimlessly around before locating the familiar path and trail leading back to the garden. A sense of relief and calm fell over him. Adam appeared rather satisfied with the outcome of his conquest. He planned to reveal to Tree and the other inhabitants his shocking new discovery. Adam intended to laugh loudly in the faces of the very creatures, and animals who had mocked and teased him. He ruminated particularly on the arrogant and cruel words of Badger who unwittingly dubbed him a bastard.

3

The Joy

It was nearly noon when Adam arrived home to the garden. He passed effortlessly through the dense wooded forest into the leading pathway of the garden. Adam entered the pasture and was instantly bombarded with gawking looks of surprise and bewilderment from the community of onlookers. They gazed on at Adam with astonishment and disbelief very much amazed and relieved by his safe return. Some creatures even began to follow behind Adam, inquiring about the creature he held and carried in his arms. Adam however mindfully arrogant declined to answer or respond to their inquiries. Adam continued his path deliberately ignorant to the growing crowd corralling behind him. Adam intentionally ignored the crowd choosing only to speak, and answer inquiries posed by his primary guardian. "Tree will know what to make of this creature." Thought Adam, "I must hurry, I can sense the creature becoming restless and will awaken soon."

Adam arrived some time shortly before Tree's post. "Hello Tree," Adam greeted. "Tree was relieved to see that Adam was safe and rejoiced by calling out his name "Adam!" She started to call out to him but stopped quickly after being confronted with uncertainty and confusion. Tree looked on puzzled at the strange load that Adam carried with him. Adam gently placed the creature down on the ground and quickly clutched the creatures' hands into his own. "What is meaning of this?" Tree demanded to know, "Who is this creature?" Tree questioned again using a firmer tone however, Adam had not answer and could only offer a shrug of his shoulders.

"Behold the creature" answered Adam, "that alarmed the garden and caused Eden great concern. I discovered the destitute creature in peril crying out for help. Yes, the terrifying noise that frightened the cowardly inhabitants was nothing more than the sound of sorrowful weeping." Adam laughed obnoxiously glaring over the faces of surrounding creatures. Tree excused Adam's childish behavior drawing her attention to the strange new creature. She studied the creature closely examining the frame, and attributes on the newly discovered being. Tree was in a sense stumped and outright baffled paralyzed somewhat in deep state of thought. She did not know how to react or what to make of the creature standing before her.

"Do you not agree?" Adam interjected thwarting Tree's concentration. "Agree what?" responded Tree, somewhat annoyed "That the creature, and I share a striking resemblance." Adam gladly surmised, before crouching down to display the physical similarities and attributes between the creature and himself. "Do you not see," Adam pleaded, "two arms, two feet, ten toes, ten fingers" and looking over the creature's protruding chest, he stopped short pondering and scratching his head "The two air pouches," Adam attempted to describe serve as flotation devices to help the creature move swiftly across the water," Tree burst into hysterical laugher, "Air pouches?" She mocked playfully with banter and amusement.

Tree smiled acknowledging Adam's innocence and ignorance regarding human anatomy and could only motion her disagreement in silence. "I can attest to witnessing this delicate creature swim amicably like a fish submerged in water," Adam advanced on, "unlike myself the creature has no lower appendage, which I believe allows the creature to swim and move much faster and efficient...." That was it, Tree had heard just about enough of Adams whimsical theories, no longer able to restrain the buildup of laughter forming deep within the cavity of her chest. Tree erupted suddenly with laughter and amusement at

Adams colorful imagination. The thought of air pouches, and missing appendages brought Tree to tears offering her much entertainment and delight.

Adam seemed confused as to the cause and source of Trees laughter, seeing as he had not made a joke. Trees infectious laughter was contagious as others watching on, began mimicking the jovial sound. Adam however was not amused and was becoming rather annoyed once again with feeling like an outsider to a collective pun and joke. He turned around to address the crowd, and just as he was about to unload on the crowd, the restless creature began to stir from behind him.

The blaring noise produced by the obnoxious crowd was loud, and rather irritating to withstand. The creature began to grow increasing uncomfortable by the noisy onlookers and clung desperately to Adam's arm trembling nervously at his side. The frail creature turned away quickly from the heckling crowd to retreat into Adam's arms. The overstimulated creature was unaccustomed to being in the presence of such wildlife with more animals gathered about the surrounding area. The startled creature was uneasy very much unsure what to expect next. The fearful creature clung desperately to Adam and looked to him to provide reassurance and safety as well as security and protection if the need came. "The creature appears to be quite fond of you." Tree observed. "Yes," Adam agreed, "But whence did the creature derive?" He posed the question to Tree hoping to receive some form of guidance or intelligence. "I do not know." Tree answered, still unsure how to respond to the presentation of Adams new companion and friend. "Speak to the creature" Tree suggested," in order to learn from where the creature originated."

Adam looked down at the creature clinging tightly to his body, "Do not be afraid," he reassured the creature describing the garden a safe place and space. "I am your friend," explained Adam, "we are all your friends," gesturing to the entire garden. Adam introduced Tree, and the many creatures that stood about. They all listened on as Adam as he shared the tale of the rescue and having to pry the creature from the clutches of the grand wall. Overtime Adam would come to tell several variations of the heralding story with much exaggeration and inconsistencies in the tale. His tales were deemed entertaining and help to elevate his reputation and rank in the garden. However, at the same time the creatures began to question the validity of Adams stories not knowing which tale to regard as fact or fiction. In the end there would be several accountings detailing the creature's arrival and sudden appearance in the kingdom.

What is your friend's name? Asked Tree. "I do not know," replied Adam, turning to the creature, "what is your name?" and just as before the creature did not have an answer unable to recall any memories. "Where did the creature come from?" Tree posed another question, "I do not know," answered Adam, turning the question over to the creature "Do you remember anything about where you came from?" Adam received the same report, "I do not know, for I cannot recall." Tree found the creatures answers to be strangely, peculiar. "It is of no use," Adam explained "as I have already posed these similar inquires."

Adam revealed the large gash on top of the creature's head and exposed the wounded area explaining how the blunt impact had forced the creatures into an amnestic and forgetful state. "I believe the creature is unable to remember much after sustaining this injury." Chattering broke out amongst the crowd; they all appeared astonished never having met a creature with no recollection or sense of identity. Tree observed the growing tension and confusion building over the unsettling crowd. "It seems to me," Tree laughing jovially, attempting to deflect the crowd's attention away from Adam and his new friend.

"Our new friend has sustained what can only be described as a head injury" Tree explained "the affliction has caused a loss of memory and ultimately the absence of the creatures identity." Tree explanation appeared to ease the mounting anxiety and look of worry drawn on their faces. Adam muttered beneath his breath at having provided similar explanation just moments before. Tree went on to solicit the crowd's participation with supporting the forgetful creature with recalling its memory. Tree requested a member to volunteer and serve as a guide in touring their beautiful garden. "Viewing the scenery and many landmarks of Eden may help to jog our visitor's memory." The thought of serving as a liaison seemed like daunting and tasking work. The crowd immediately turned their faces withdrawing their initial interest in the new creature.

"Who is willing to volunteer?" Tree posed candidly to the group of surveying animals pretentiously grazing the floors. The crowd began to shy away, looking around darting glances back and forth at each other all while avoiding direct eye contact. "Is there no one willing to spare a moment of their time to help accompany our new visitor on a tour around the garden?" Tree posed the suggestion predicting with accuracy the outcome and response to the request. She understood the mindset and behavior of the inhabits of the garden. The subservient creatures were loyal to a degree and would only obey if strongly encouraged, however Tree was being intentionally passive in enlisting the services of the unenthusiastic crowd.

Just as Tree imagined not a single creatures stepped forth to accept the task. Many of the animals were already beginning to disperse taking their leave to attend to other affairs . "No worries," Adam assured, "I can manage the tour without assistance, besides who else knows these gardens better than me." "Alright," Tree responded smiling impishly with beaten brows. "Just be safe, and do not trail too far, and be back in time for supper." Adam happily accepted the numerous prerequisites posed by his loving matriarch. All to secure the chance and opportunity to escort and accompany his new friend. "Yes, Tree," answered Adam with youthful exuberance "yes, to it all." He grabbed the creature by the hand and together they begin their tour of the botanical estate.

They two strolled through the garden for some time walking together in silence. "It must be difficult," said Adam breaking the awkward tension. "Not being able to remember," "I do not recall the details of who I am" answered the creature, "but I do hold faint thoughts; images and moments that's replay over in my mind. Adam listened on with growing interest to the creature. "What sort of images?" He asked eager to learn more about his new friend. The creature despite prior reservations was slowly beginning to warm up to Adam growing more comfortable in his company and presence.

Adam channeled a sense of safety, and genuine care in his demeanor that enabled the creature to open-up and share. "I see images," said the creature "of a small child left alone by its keeper. It seems its proprietor has forgotten about the small child. Feeling abandoned, and forgotten the child grows up living its days in pity and hopelessness. The child falls pitifully into an endless voyage of wanderlust in desperate search of purpose and belonging. The journey however seems endless leaving the child's feet course, and calloused, its heart cold and bitter plagued with sorrow and loneliness." The creature eerie tale appeared to somewhat dampen the mood however drew Adam's attention.

"Many nights the child stayed up pondering as to the reason for the absence of its creator, desiring nothing more than a sense of security, and belonging. Often the child wondered as to the whereabouts of its maker. The child was raised in total isolation with no sense of creed or guild to proclaim alliance or allegiance" Adam was taken aback by the creatures moving description and strongly empathized with the child in the story. In Adams eyes the creature was professing a truth that resonated and aligned with his own personal experiences. The emotional story was triggering and somewhat troubling to hear. It managed to stir up unwanted feelings and emotions in Adam. The dormant feelings which Adam believed had long been silenced were beginning to resurface to plague his mind and heart. Tears spewed down the side of creature face. 'I cannot say for sure, but I believe that very child to be me." Adam appeared astonished by the sudden revelation in creature's tale.

"I yearned for my creator's regard and affection however unrequited were those feelings which burned deep within me like ember. I eventually exhausted the flame and gave up all hope to accept my despairing fate. But after meeting you," The creature stopped to look at Adam, peering directly into his eyes. "I confess a growing fondness in your presence, you evoke strong feelings within me. These emotions I can never describe but find that it intensifies whenever you are near." Adam was unable to disguise the joy produced by the creatures' flattery. The admission produced a large grin over his face which he was unable to disguise. Adam blushed in response to the compliment finding himself very much pleased by what he was hearing. "If not for your rescue," The creature continued, "I would be lost forever in the barren abyss of darkness. I was eternally damned, confined without refuge, expected to live the remainder of my existence in isolation and solitude."

"Please no more." Adam interjected, having heard enough of the melancholy story. He appeared uneasy with the dreary tale and urged that uncomfortable story be concluded. Adam had been listening closely and was satisfied if not moved by the intense heartfelt admission. "I know the feeling all too well," Adam reflected, "having long endured several decades of isolation. I have lived alone unmatched and unpaired in the absence of a mate and companion."

Adam rested his hand on the creatures' shoulders, and softly caressed the side of the creature's face against his own. "New friend, Adam continued, "if you offer me your hand in companionship, I will return the same degree of loyalty back to you." The creature and Adam shared a similar mindset of ideals and values which mirrored if not reflected their deep longing desire for mutual devotion, and companionship.

Over the course of time Adam and the creatures bond grew stronger. Their friendship lasted many moons, enduring through passing seasons. The couple soon became the most popular pairing in the kingdom. They were greeted, and celebrated, by all the creatures that encountered them on their walks. Adam had discovered his soul mate with whom he happily explored his emotions and mutual fondness. In essence the creature taught Adam how to feel and in return Adam offered the creature the safety and security of Eden as their home.

Adam and his companion were often spotted walking and frolicking about in the garden. The two seemed inseparable and very much in love as evidenced by their public display, and acts of affection. The creature gave Adam a sense of peace and inner calm. Adam cherished the fact that that he no longer felt isolated finally having found a friend to call his own. Whenever Adam felt overwhelmed or faced bouts of sadness for reasons dire or trivial, he found that his partner was the perfect companion to confide and unload his troubles. The creature would eventually learn how to sooth Adam and relieve him of stress and worries. The art of seduction had become the creature's therapeutic hold and preferred method of practice. Adam's anxiety and tension seemed to dissolve under the tender care and treatment of his partner. The intimate routine often concluded with Adam feeling quelled of his worries, and emotionally pacified unable to recall the source of his tension and frustration.

Tree saw firsthand the profound change and impact the creature had over Adam. She took special notice to the improvement of his attitude and overall mood since the introduction of his companion and friend. The creature's presence seemed to provide Adam a sense of joy and bliss that was shared between him and the creature. Tree watched on carefully observing as Adam's and the creature's relationship developed over time, growing from budding seeds into flourishing plants. Their relationship continued to mature and blossom until eventually reaching the point of mutual partnership. Tree grew fond of Adam's new friend, and one day expressed her joy to Adam, "I am glad that you have found your help mate." She remarked, "Yes," Adam answered, "I can solemnly agree, I have never been more enthralled by the presence of another creature or being." "This is without question."

Tree continued in her observation, "I find that any creature with the ability to wield such joy and evoke delight into another's life must undoubtably be a blessing of some sorts. The creature seems if nothing else to be a tokened offering placed in the garden by the most high and favorable God." "I believe you are right," acknowledged Adam giving favor and praise to his father and creator, "No creature or being should be left to exist alone unpaired and unmatched." Adam felt a sense of guilt for his insensitivity looking over at Tree, "Do you feel alone?" Adam asked the swelling question catching Tree somewhat off-guard. "Me, why not at all," Tree stammered to disclose, "I do not feel alone, I have you, and the many friends and inhabitants of the garden. "I guess you are right." Adam agreed right before running off to frolic and play with his new friend.

The beloved couple were the admired and highly regarded as the most joyful creatures residing in all of Eden. As it commonly occurs in instances of cohabitation the pair would soon receive blessed and profound news. The creature with whom Adam had befriended was now with child. The couple would rejoice in their discovery considering the news to be an omen of good fortune. Initially they shared the good news with Tree, but before long the rumors of the couple's good fortune surged throughout the kingdom spreading like wildfire. Tree would later come to orchestrate a surprise reveal to officiate the couple's celebratory announcement.

One warm day as Adam and his companion sat lazily beneath the shade of Tree's branches. Creatures from around the kingdom began to gather appearing suddenly before the young couple. The festive spirit and honor of tradition brought the garden together to celebrate the fortunate news. The visitors arrived in groves to offer their respect and share in thoughtful prayer over the soon to be triad. Many of the creatures traveled long distances bearing exotic and tasty foods. They showered the couple in sweet delectables given to Adam and his partner as palpable gifts to celebrate and honor their good fortune. The festivities lasted for some time and would have continued through the day had it been for the dwindling sun setting the path of the evening sky. As the light began to descend slowly retreating softly beneath the horizon so did the visitors begin to make their way. The receding sunlight served as a helpful indicator to the group of wild party animals that the festivities were over. The creatures who remained in attendance were very much exhausted and fatigued. Full of ale and merriment the creatures began to slowly make their departure. But not before congratulating the two lovers embarking the path of family and union.

4

———————

The Return

These were the happiest times for Adam and his companion in the Garden. They lived happily in cohabitation enjoying the wondrous splendors of Eden. The hospitality, and kindness demonstrated by the citizens of the garden made the land an inviting place to live. Tree managed to maintain order and structure throughout Eden fulfilling her governing role and title. She was celebrated favorably and regarded highly by all the tenants and inhabitants of Eden.

One day while attending to her natural duties, God appeared to Tree. His sudden and unexpected appearance took Tree by surprise. "Tree my good friend," God eagerly announced, "It is nice to see that you are well. It seems your coat of bark has thickened rather nicely since our last meet. I like what you have done with the place, you've outdone yourself in transforming this small botanical garden into a luxurious paradise." Tree was still in shock, somewhat stunned and confused by the king's unexpected arrival. "Thank you, my lord," she managed finally to offer a response. "Tree, it seems that I have succeeded in cleansing my castle of those treacherous angels. A most inglorious battle ensued before their defeat. But in the end, I could not bear to destroy that of which I had created." God took a long-poised breath clenching his fist over his lips. "Sadly, I could not do it. Those foolish misguided angels deserved pity and mercy more than total annihilation. In believing so, I chose to cast them into the deepest nether regions to live out the rest of eternity. Restricted to the under-

33

world their wings serve no significance other than a reminder of their treachery and treason."

Tree celebrated in the triumphant tale of the king's report. She glorified in her mind the victorious battle waged and rejoiced at the glorious outcome. "This is most excellent news." Tree remarked "Adam will be delighted to hear of your return." "Adam" repeated God appearing confused. "Why, yes." Tree responded jovially, "Your son, has been assigned a worldly name. "Indeed." God was amused, "Well then, I am ready to take my son, Adam home with me into the heavens where he shall reign as a testimonial trophy to greatest war ever waged." Tree without haste did as the king commanded and immediately summoned the surrounding creatures to search the garden for Adam and implore his hasty return home. The creatures scattered and scurried moving quickly into the woods to seek out and find Adam. It wasn't long before they located Adam resting peacefully in the fields. The creatures bombarded Adam eager to deliver the news of his summons.

Adam appeared shortly stepping forth from behind the bushy jungle, he was accompanied by his swollen companion. "Who is this creature?" God demanded to know speaking in a rather harsh and unpleasant tone, "What is the meaning of this Tree?" Tree responded with confusion unable to comprehend the exact issue that perplexed and vexed the king. "What do you mean your highness," Tree replied "why, the creature before you is none other than, Adam. I admit that he has grown much since you last placed eyes on him. And as you can see Adam has matured beyond the scope of my care, and now enjoys the company of another."

A loud snap of thunder exploded from the sky as thick bogs of clouds began to form dimming the lit sky. The calm winds began to blow wildly picking up force and intensity. The creatures of Eden were thrown instantly into a state of panic and dismal confusion. The startling sounds of roaring thunder and howling winds terrified the creatures sending them into a state of confusion and panic. A sudden brisk chill and change in the weather served as a cause for great concern. Responding to imminent threat and danger all the creatures began to panic and flee desperate to escape the hostile area. The peaceful paradise had never experienced such terrifying conditions and were vaguely unfamiliar to the fierce climate of forceful winds. The frightened creatures sought refuge retreating quickly into the confines and safety of their homes and dwellings.

God was upset and very much displeased by the ordeal. He reflected a look of irritation that displayed his disappoint with Tree, Adam and the entire garden. "Who is responsible for this creature that stands before me in the shadow of my creation." "Your highness" Tree responded "Adam discovered the creature near the outskirts of the grand wall. We welcomed the creature into Eden under the assumption that the creature was a gift to Adam. We all assumed the creature was bestowed to Adam, and Eden by our gracious and most honorable host. I pray that you heard Adams cries of loneliness, and finally answered his call and provided to him a companion and mate..." "Do not be ridiculous," God interjected responding crudely, "I did not create this forsaken creature!" God renounced the creature with extreme pride and prejudice. "I will not accept responsibility for a being that is not my own."

God peered closely at the creature his eyes following every inch of the creature frame and design. The creature was uneasy, somewhat unnerved by the piercing gaze of the unknown stranger. "What is going on," the creature questioned looking to Adam to provide an answer, "who is he?" asked his frightened companion whimpering and clinging nervously to his side. Adam did not answer but stood entranced and dazed, rather appalled by the crude and egregious behavior of their proprietor and host. God had seen enough, wearing a look of disgust and disapproval of Adam's mate. Sensing growing tension emanating from the stranger the creature clung tighter to Adam for reassurance. "It appears that the war waged in heaven has managed to somehow to spill down into Eden," The king massaged the back of his neck appearing rather exhausted and overcome with disbelief. God heaved a gust of air into his lungs, the hefty sigh signified with clarity his disappointment and growing frustration with present situation.

"This creature is not a product of my construct," God explained, "and must undoubtedly be forged by the hands of my nemesis through the dark arts and practice alchemy." Adam, and Tree looked at one another seemingly confused by the information being gathered. God continued, "This ensnaring drifter was fashioned without my knowledge or consent, most likely placed here by those devious angels as a contingent measure. A desperate final attempt to foil my grand scheme and plan. But I will not allow them to win." God begrudgingly admitted.

God lifted his arm pointing outward, he waved his finger in direction of the nimble creature. The simple gesture lifted Adams companion aimlessly into the air. God rotated the creature in the air examining the creature closely as if mystified by the creature's contemporary build and framework. Seeing his companion being twirled about in the air upset Adam, who felt compelled to speak out on his partners behalf. He stepped forth and demanded that his companion be released from his hold. "Please put my partner down!" Adam pleaded but found his voice held no weight or value. God was thoroughly engrossed in the study of the strange creature paying little mind to Adams pleading request. God looked closely over the creature observably intrigued by the creature's unique attributes and design.

"Those wicked angels," God renounced, shaking his head disagreeably, "somehow managed to spawn and conjure a being nearly identical to that of my creation. Had I known beforehand the evidence of their misdeeds were housed here in Eden, I would have confronted those traitors publicly and avoided the pro-longed and rather lengthy trial." The judgement and sentencing for acts of contempt and treason fell upon disciplinarian hands of the king. God began to regret his decision to demonstrate mercy and pity over his enemies rather than imploring his wrath. "To hell with them." God declared, "I will however commend their novice attempt to duplicate my most prized and greatest work."

Adam was becoming increasingly irritated, that his request was being ignored. Witnessing the disrespect his mate was enduring only helped to fuel his already hot and boiling temper. "Stop it now!" Adam demanded in a firm and commanding tone. "I am Adam, the proud prince of Eden, and I presume you are God, our divine landlord and king." God was surprised, unsure how to react to Adams informal demeanor. He appeared ignorantly unaware of the fact that he was now addressing his father and creator.

"I recognize very well, who you are Adam" God announced, "though I am a bit irritated to find that you do not know who I am." God shot a sharp glance in Trees direction that stung its intended mark. "Please your highness," Adam pleaded faithfully, "do not pass judgment over Tree for she is my dearest friend. Tree is without a doubt the kindest, and noblest of all the creatures you have ever created." Adam grasped the hands of his companion and gently pulled the creature back down to the ground. "I feared this moment would one day arrive," continued Adam, "I often fantasized over the day we would eventually come to meet. I recited over and over in my mind the many things that I would say and do if the moment would ever arrive. In playing out various scenarios, I explored endless possibilities in which the outcome would conclude with a fierce and fiery confrontation. However, I never expected that we would meet in the presence of my swollen and fragile companion for which I find myself entirely disarmed and compelled to offer my deepest apologies for any offense or wrongdoing."

Tree looked on at Adam strangely perplexed and confused, "But how did he know?" She probed her thoughts recalling having given specific instructions that no one should disclose or release such pertinent information. "Tree has never spoken a word of your name to me," Adam continued, "but still I managed to learn of your existence and the sacred connection and bond that we share. I discovered that you were my creator simply by observing the behaviors of the creatures of the jungle. Seeing how they treated me favorably praising my presence publicly solely on the premise and knowledge that I was a unique and special child."

"At other times, while unaware of my presence the very same creatures would ridicule, and joke openly at my expense. While grazing over the pastures, huddled together in communion they shared tales and secrets of my origin and lineage. Seldomly was I not the topic and subject of their discourse. Whenever my name was brought to discussion, the creatures rarely passed on the opportunity to offer their candid views and honest opinions of my measure and worth."

"I may have been at fault for snooping and prying into the private discourse and affairs of others. However, I could not resist the temptation to hear their thoughts and opinions of me. I immediately regretted the act unprepared for the chaffing criticism that followed. They spoke harshly of me and stoned me with indignation. They snagged my insecurities without care or discernment. They unraveled me to the point that I became undone. I fell ill to their thoughts and was ultimately poisoned by their negative perception of me. I found myself consumed with bitterness and anguish sunken beyond the lowly depths of my ego."

Their taunting words and mocking banter aimed to poke fun at the odds and likelihood of fulfilling my assignment. A fate and destiny the likes of which was hidden from me." Adam paused for a moment, inhaling deeply, "They made me question myself like never before." Adam confessed mournfully, "On that day something happened to me, or rather something changed within me that greatly impacted my outlook and view of the world. Some days I can still hear their insidious laughter echoing in my thoughts gnawing away at my esteem and confidence. Overhearing the creatures describing me in such a deplorable fashion has since affected me to point that I began to second guess and question the quality of my own capabilities."

Adam spoke clearly in an unwavering and distinguished tone. He shared his feelings and emotions without hesitation or reservation. Adam was no longer the soft-spoken docile child that God had tenderly crafted, instead he was now primed, and peaked in height and stature. Despite his growth and brave disposition Adam found himself standing timidly before the shadow of his father and creator.

"In your extended of absence, Tree has managed to raise me well, fulfilling her assignment in caring and ensuring my safety. Tree helped me grow into the man standing before you. It is to her with whom I pledge my allegiance. She has taught me compassion and empathy showing me unconditional love, all these traits which I committed my life to upholding." Looking directly into the frightened face of his mate, quaking nervously, "The creature you describe before me is not a being crafted of sin, or forged by evil design. How can it be, when very same creature you belittle, and degrade has helped me to find purpose by adding meaning to my life. I had never experienced such joy and ecstasy and never imagined that such a state could exist before our introduction. My partner has taught me affection and companionship in a way that no other creature could. We agreed to merge our journeys to forge a lifelong voyage and path of self-discovery and love."

Adam was beginning to grow rather tearful and remorseful. "I do not expect you to understand" he continued, "the trails of solitude, and isolation for which I have endured. The haunting emotions of loneliness, and anguish that taunted me from the day I learned of your existence." Adam sheltered his companion shielding the creature safely behind his body, He was ready to protect the creature from any swift attacks or retaliation made by the king.

As a child Adam often received reprimands from Tree for his disruptive outbursts. He was encouraged to refrain from such hostile conduct and behavior. However, now Tree was restraining the urge to interrupt and apply corrective action to Adam's unruly behavior. Tree did not stir or speak out to condemn Adam finding no fault in him expressing his pent-up feelings . Tree of all creatures understood the insufferable emotions which Adam harbored and suppressed inside slowly unfolding. God felt confronted forced to face the flood of childhood emotions after triggering Adams dormant insecurities. The livid emotions buried deep within Adam were beginning to surface. Adam evoked feelings of resentment and abandonment after recalling the anguish and resentment experienced as a youth. He was prepared for confrontation and directed his gaze back towards the absentee parent who had finally returned to pick up and retrieve his son like simple produce after a successful harvest. The manifestation of Adam's unbridled emotions was now becoming overwhelmingly difficult to circumvent. Adam struggled to restrain his emotions and control his feelings. He appeared rather upset and annoyed with his creator began to speak recklessly.

"Tell me father," Adam demanded suddenly, "am I such a pathetic creature, so unworthy of your love that you chose to abandon me?" God could not believe the audacity of Adam's embittered remarks filled with contentious disrespect. "The burning desires of my youth that once flared at the thought of us one day meeting have since subsided." Adams voice gained momentum, growing bolder and more hostile in tone. He voiced with ample passion the harbored feelings of contempt and anguish he held for his father. God listened on to the painful outcries of his son, and creation. The unwavering sense of abandonment felt by Adam's in his childhood suddenly eclipsed his mind and thoughts. Adam found himself suddenly reliving the degradation and uncertainty of his youth. He recalled the pain of having his basic emotional needs neglected by a remote and unbothered founder.

These grievances and more Adam spewed carelessly at his father. However, God was not upset or offended, he understood fully that Adam was simply venting his pent-up frustrations. The king however frowned against Adam's strong use of language and unflattering remarks. Adam continued to fling forth several harsh insults, and words at his maker. Tree watched on from above growing rather concerned if not worried that Adam's insolent behavior would not be tolerated for much longer. God listened patiently trying desperately not to take any offense to the misgivings of Adam's foul and slanderous assault. Adam showed very little regard and respect to the honored guest standing before him. In return God faced his tormentor demonstrating a degree of indifference toward his subject.

The awkward moment drew increasingly more tense between the two. Adam, and God were defiantly matched and willfully opposed. They stared down one another with sharp and piercing gazes. God felt affronted by his creations conduct and was very much displeased with Adam's deplorable display of arrogance and hubris. God considered for a brief instance the idea of unleashing his wrath over Adam, believing that a firm slap or thumping would help correct his attitude and behavior possibly jogging some sense back into him. It was undoubtedly true that Adam's belligerent reproach deserved disciplinary actions, however despite the strong urge, God was reluctant to smite his son for the minor infraction of speaking openly and sharing his deepest feelings and thoughts out loud.

Adam's eyes began to water and fill as he voiced his anguish. His mate in seeing Adam in distress quickly stepped forth to offer comfort and reassurance. The warm soothing touch of his companion was enough to draw Adam's attention away from his troubles. "Be still my love," whispered Adams mate, "for if he is indeed your creator and father then honor and respect is due." The tender words of his mate instantly disarmed Adam calling him to consider the extent of his behavior against his father. Turning to his partner and locking eyes Adam could see the look of fear twinkling beneath the soft brows of his dear beloved. Realizing that his mate was uneasy being present amongst the turmoil of such a heated and intense family feuding and confrontation.

"I am sorry," Adam, apologized to his mate "It was not my intentions for you to see me like this, but..." His words were stopped short with a delicate finger pressed against his lip. "Do not be sorry my love but be yourself, the Adam that I have come to know and love and proudly call my partner." In response to receiving such affection and praise, Adam's companion was able to defuse his anguish and awaken within him a hopeful and positive conclusion to the hostile standoff.

Peering directly into the eyes of his mate, Adam could feel the tender love and admiration that his mate regarded for him. He had never experienced such strong feelings of passion and longing for any other creature. Adam could not imagine or foresee a future and life without his companion and mate. "I know what I must do," Adam explained turning his attention back over to God, "I am ready to accept my destiny." he announced stepping forward before his mate. Adam demonstrated his sense of nobility by offering to accept and uphold the sacred role and prophecy that was assigned to him.

"I am willing to go forth with you into realms of heaven and accept my destiny and rightful place at your side. I will serve as your pupil and swear my unyielding allegiance to your noble cause and campaign," Adams offer brought God much joy, and had he stopped at this point a possible reconciliation could have established between the two. But sadly, this was not the case. The heightened feelings of bliss and joy experienced by the king would soon transform back into feeling of anguish and remorse. "I will only travel with you to heaven," Adam declared, "on one condition, that you allow for the safe passage for both Tree, and my beloved companion to accompany us as well. This is my only request."

Adams demands enraged the king beyond the brinks of frustration and contempt. God was fed up with Adams reckless attitude, and baseless demands. The sky began to dim as dark clouds began to form across the sky. The gloomy eclipse cast a shadowy veil over the land that covered the garden entirely. The dwindling sun and its powerful rays struggled to penetrate the thick fog of clouds restricting light from entering the garden. The unlit garden was now engulfed in shadowy darkness

A gust of wind suddenly emerged. The swift and unwavering wind blew with fierce intensity thrusting dirt and debris into the air. Adam and his mate were forced to hold onto Tree's base and body to avoid being hurled into the air. The forceful winds gradually increased, stretching and snapping away twigs, and limbs off Tree's body. Hearing the painful snapping of Tree's limbs being fractured and torn apart was a rather unnerving and traumatic experience. Adam and his companion watched on helplessly as boughs and branches were being severed and removed from Tree's body. A second branch much bulkier than the last bough fell suddenly crashing dangerously close to Adam and his mate. The fluttering leaves of the fallen branch were quickly stripped and carried away by the ravishing wind. The savage winds raged wildly gathering small particles of twigs and sticks into the air. Adam had never witnessed the destructive force of nature until now. He was experiencing first-hand the pain and impact of unstable climate. There was an onslaught of debris and fragments hurling around him and his mate. Adam tried the best he could to shield and cover his delicate mate from enduring the blistering pain of the abusive wind.

The unsettling winds disturb the three body of rivers in Eden causing great peril and concern amongst aquatic creatures. The water creatures drew alarm at the disturbing change in weather conditions. The once quiet and still rivers now raged rapidly with an eruption of waves crashing the banks and shores. The sound of booming thunder began to erupt from the dark sky; the bolstering sound cracked loudly like a loud a whip snapping through the air. The loud explosion of sound erupting from the sky were useful in helping to detour any observers or lingering onlookers. Strobes of light began to emerge and flicker from the bowels of the rumbling rolling clouds. Suddenly, without warning a bolt of lightning darted down from the sky. The impact of the fiery thunderbolt ignited immediately upon impact resulting in a fiery blaze. Adam instantly recounted images from the frightening nightmares he disclosed and shared with Tree during his childhood. "The scene from my dreams." Adam struggled to communicate while facing the brutal conditions. The growing flames fed easily from the debris of twigs and dried leaves scattered about by the wild winds.

The temperature of the environment began to raise slowly with the rapid growth of fire spreading around them. An impeding sense of danger was universally acknowledged by all the creatures watching pitifully their precious home and garden being demolished and engulfed by flames. The few creatures who remained to spectate immediately regretted the decision in doing so and began searching desperately for a means of escape. The others who were fortunate enough to escape retreated home to their dwellings. The unfortunate group of creatures who found themselves trapped off by the flames and cried out to Adam to rescue and save them from their impeding demise. Those that were fortunate to escape the fiery blaze furthered their distance only to turn around and serve as spectators from a safe distance. The smoldering clouds continued cover the sky as the rumbling thunder produced bolts of lightning like raindrops. "Please stop!" pleaded Adam's mate, crying out woefully. "You are destroying everything." The creature cries went scarcely acknowledged. Adam echoed his mate's plea. "Yes, please stop you are destroying our home." God ignored their request dismissing their pouring outcries. In his current state of wrath and indifference God appeared deafened by his temper and blinded by his fury and rage. He simply refused to hear out or listen to any more their ridiculous pleas. God's fiery temper would not allow him to negotiate with the likes and demands of his arrogant subjects.

Please, my king!" Tree cried out, "I beg that you end your path of destruction. I understand your anguish with Adam, but must the entire Eden suffer so unjustly. Look around at your loyal subjects who now crouch and quiver with fear. Look at my broken limbs lying about on the ground, see the dents, and holes you have unearthed. Please my lord, cease your reign of fury over us." Trees sobering words began to slowly settle over the king's mind, calling for an end to the violent lightning storm. God paused a moment to look over the faces of surrounding creatures watching him in terror and dismay. He found himself being confronted with looks of worry, and confusion leering back at him. The petrified creatures had been watching on in disbelief at the chaotic wrath of their God. Many were witnessing for the first time the extent of their king power and temperance.

"You are right Tree," God admitted, "however I cannot just stand by idly as l this treacherous ploy unfolds before my eyes. God turned his attention to Adam, speaking earnestly as possible. "Son, this creature only seeks to corrupt and disrupt you from fulfilling your prophecy and purpose. "Directing his gaze over at Adams mate, "This creature harbors insidious intentions and is only attempting to manipulate and use you to get back into heaven." God rested his arm on Adams shoulder, "My son, it has become plainly obvious that the creature has corrupted you. You have been entranced somewhat placed under an intimate spell the likes of which has blinded you to the foreseeable truth. The creature carries a hidden agenda seeking only for a means to an end. The creature is attempting to breach the boarders and gates of heaven. I simply cannot allow such a creature to deploy havoc and chaos in my kingdom. This creatures design was not forged or molded by my hands, and as such the being cannot be entirely trusted. The familiar creature retains somewhat of your likeness and identity however do not be fooled. As your creator and protector, I cannot allow this creature to further taint and impurify your soul."

"Do not curse my beloved," Adam shouted in defense of his companion. He had heard enough slander and was now upset and enraged by God's admissions, "My partner was not molded from sin, nor will our child and offspring carry any trace of impurity or evil." Adams hot temper boiled over into fuming aguish, he refused to believe that a creature as tender and kind as his mate could be crafted by villainous hands. God appeared stunned to discover that the creature Adam called his mate was with child. He threw up his arms to demonstrate his frustration and surrender. "I am spoiled," God cried out, "my divine plan has been demolished. "You are my son, my child, my greatest achievement. You were designed to be a divine and great creature not a being of domestication. I have always loved you and planned to make up for my absence by gifting you the throne of heaven. However, the impregnable news of a possible addition has scornfully affected me beyond the point of disappointment in your decision to stand alongside evil."

Throughout time and the existence no one had ever witnessed or seen firsthand the flushed and flustered face of God. The rare but seldom sighting was compelling. An upsetting image of their king saddled in disappointment and damp with moist tears. Thick clouds began to suddenly emerge followed by a shower of rain., The raindrops helped to mask and cover God's flowing tears. The cool wet rain helped to quench the sweltering land, extinguishing the traces of burning ember that remained. The heavy rain began to pick up force and intensity with the help of the gusty winds. The pricking sound of heavy raindrops could be heard beating down on the ground, and against the naked bodies of Adam and his companion.

The defenseless couple held onto one another in a futile attempt to shield each other from the piercing rain. "Please, forgive us," Adam's mate began to plea, "have mercy on our souls." The tearful outcry began to resemble that of a heartfelt confession. "You are wrong my lord," corrected the creature, "I do not know who my creator is, nor do I retain any memory or knowledge of the hands that helped to craft and mold me. I have no idea what evil is, nor will I choose to associate myself with such a notion. This encounter will forever be engrained as my first meeting and interaction with the forces of evil." The howling winds blew louder in response to flagrant remark made by Adam's partner. The swift moved quickly to attack the creature by smothering its face. Adam stretched his arms out and managed to pull his companion back into his arms. In the face of present circumstances, the sanctuary of Adams arms was the safest hiding place. Adam sought desperately to shield and protect the womb of his mate from the tumultuous climate of harsh wind and rain.

"I refuse to let evil back into my kingdom!" God proclaimed vengefully, "My mate is not evil!" Adam retaliated, enduring the pang of heavy rainfall beating hard against his back. The painful sound of moaning began to escape his sealed and somewhat pressured lips. "Stop it please!!!" Adams mate cried out hysterically, "you are hurting Adam can you not see that he is…" God silenced the creature with a simple snap of his fingers, transforming the creature into inaudible mute. The creature was no longer able to voice its opinions or produce any coherent sounds of speech.

"What is the matter," God teased childishly. "Silence seems to suit you well." Adams mate reacted with muffled panic and rage, confronted with the sudden inability to speak out or produce any audible sound. "What have you done to my mate ," Adam, demanded to know in a loud roaring voice. "Why is it that my partner no longer able to communicate or call out to me," Adam was troubled and not exactly sure how to react. "Return my beloved partners voice" Adam demanded growing increasingly impatient with the king's deplorable act and sudden imposition.

"Can you not see my son," God attempted to explain, "that I am saving you? Trust in me and have faith that I do only what is best for my creations. You are my son, and I am your father. Honor me by pledging your allegiance my desire and will. Accept and fulfill your prophetic assignment and destiny." Adam was irritated and refused to listen to Gods reasoning growing somewhat deaf and intolerant beneath the weight of sorrow and anguish. "You are not my father!" Adam discharged suddenly, "you are just my creator." The garden suddenly fell into barren silence. God was stunned by the unexpected declaration, unprepared for the candid honesty of his Adam's admission. But before God could react or respond, Adam persisted.

"The title and deed of father is the crowning title that a child or beneficiary bestows on their benefactor. Adam's voice was brisk, "It is a sounding badge; a merit of opulence." Adam looked up at Tree recalling all that she had done and sacrificed to ensure not only his survival but happiness as well. "The provisional role of caring for another life is no easy task, however the challenge gathers bountiful spoils." Adam, fell silent, hesitating for a moment to speak. "Heaven must truly be a paradise; a luxuriously wonderful place worthy of justifying the reason a creator would choose to abandon their own creation and child in a foreign world.

God stopped listening feeling somewhat slighted by the offense. He declared to having heard enough of Adams nonsensical ramblings. "How, dare you," God scolded, "speak to me with such an insolent tone of disrespect. His temper boiled over festering into bouts of anger and rage. God was astonished by Adam's boisterous arrogance; the extent of his hubris remarks appeared impactful. "You could never begin to imagine the many sacrifices that I bore to ensure that you were well kept. I made assurances that you would be granted the bountiful spoils and comforts of easy living. Tell me son, was I wrong for giving you a luxurious life by placing you in the sanctuary of this bountiful paradise and garden. In my absence I ensured that you were kept safe and well off. I made sure that you needed for nothing and was refused nothing. You grew up privileged never knowing the pains and aches of hunger, and uncertainty. You were shielded from despair and gloom provided a carefree life removed of troubles and worries." God was undeniably upset by Adams staggering admission.

"And yet, you speak as though you were tossed away and abandoned left to starve with no sight of hope. It has become apparently clear that you have taken for granted the provisional paradise and oasis I have afforded you. You have forgotten that you have benefitted as a tenant and resident in this gardened paradise that you regard as your home. God felt affronted by Adam's indignation and declared, "This world which I crafted with your comfort and safety in mind will no longer house you."

Adam reacted with confusion to the sudden declaration appearing somewhat baffled. "Eden will no longer shelter and protect you from the inequities and uncertainties of life." God declared, "you will witness first-hand the absence of my grace and good fortune over you. The bountiful splendors which you have unwittingly benefitted and taken for granted will no longer assure your thriving survival."

"But now we will explore first-hand the strength of your autonomy and practice of self-determination. You will now tread freely though the course of an untamed and merciless world filled with challenges and adversity at every turn and footing. This will now be your new life, and though it saddens me deeply to offer such harsh sentencing it is my sound hope that your resilience will overcome the hurdles and pitfalls of this world while retaining your humility and integrity." God shed a final tear for his son, "In time you will come to see the truth revealed confirming all that I have declared to you." God shunned Adam turning away from him and his sorry companion. God turned to face the watchful eyes of the gazing public before making the important announcement. "Let it be known that from this day," God proclaimed with an air of clarity, "that Adam and his mate are hence forth exiled. They will be banished forever banned from entering the sanctuary of the garden."

The command came as a shocking surprise to the many inhabitants listening. The creatures could only respond with looks of terror and despair. "Please sire!" pleaded Tree, attempting to ease and sooth her masters temper, however the king would not be detoured from completing his sanction. God shifted his gaze peering closely at Adam and his mate, "Outcasts!" he cursed the pair shouting brazenly. "You must now leave the sacred garden and never return." Adam and his petrified mate were entirely consumed with fear. They fearful couple were unsure how to proceed and stood frozen paralyzed with confusion at God's defeating request. God seemed to grow rather impatient with the defiant couple observing their hesitation to leave Eden as instructed. God extended his arms toward the air, drawing down from the sky two beaming blades of light. "You could have easily become a God like I," explained the king. "But you allowed yourself to fall to the perverse allure of evil." Adam was confused, and rather unsure what to expect next. "And go where?" Adam cried out, pleading heartedly "I know no other home than Eden." However, the treacherous act would not be tolerated or accepted by the likes of the proud king.

It was too much too late for Adam, there were no words or appeals that would offset the king from moving forward with his plan. The two fluorescent blades began to hum and glow brighter. The kings' eyes were firmly fixed on Adams face waiting for the perfect opportunity to steal a moment of his gaze. Adam finally looked up and locked eyes with his father for an intense and heart-wrenching stare down. God looked drudgingly into the face of his sacred creation. Strangely the king found himself touched and saddened with fraught at the conclusion of his hopeful endeavors and dreams. "A child is the ultimate form of sacrifice," God warned, "as you will soon come to discover., The tender act of childrearing will require mass amounts of energy and life force. The task of caring for new life will consume you and eventually overshadow your very existence. Your soaring ascension into fatherhood will eventually become your spiraling descent and fall from greatness. Eventually you will come to experience the bitter resentment and exhaustion of inequivalent exchange." The beams of light slowly began to spin like propellers cutting effortlessly through the air. The blades spun with enough force and speed to form a hefty gust resembling that of the natural winds. The speed and intensity of the spinning blades synchronized in an endless cycle growing stronger with every completion. The wreckage off limbs and earthly debris began to slowly tumble and fly away. Twigs and small sticks began flying past Adam and his mate as they held on to one another. Adam used his body to shield his mate from the path of projectiles and flying fragments being carried through the air.

The ultra bright light beams burned with intensity; the powerful propellers blew like giant fans panning over and around the defenseless couple. Adam soon found himself facing the full force and intensity of the staggering wind. He braved the winds as best as he could shoving and pushing back with as much heart and strength as he could muster. "Resist as best as you can," God warned, "but eventually the wrathful winds will overpower you." The struggling couple attempted to protest their unfair eviction. The observable mistreatment of being forcibly thrown out and removed from Eden was without indignation. Adam and his mate clasped tightly to one another clutching desperately against the wild and powerful winds. Despite their commendable efforts, Adam and his mate were unmatched against the mystical forces driving them out. Adam's mate took a misstep and accidentally lost footing and was instantly lifted and carried into the air. Adam quickly reached outward and managed to grasp hold of his mate's arm. His remaining arm held firmly, gripped over a protruding root that suddenly appeared bulging out from beneath the ground.

Tree was overwhelmed with grief watching on helplessly at the deplorable eviction taking place. She wanted to speak out on Adams behalf but was unable to muster the courage. Tree was fearful that her advocacy would be received with undeserving backlash. The lit beams were now spinning at full speed. Adam struggled to hold firm to the base and handle of the protruding root. He could feel his mates grasp slowly slipping from his grips. Adam understood that a decision needed to be made however with little room for hesitation he settled on a decision. He released his grip on the root and together he and his mate were thrown into the air. The forceful winds carried the couple off chauffeuring them through the sky a great distance beyond the range of their home. Looking below Adam could see the entire garden, and quickly recognized the direction that they were being led. Adam had become rather familiar with geography of Eden and recognized the landmarks trailing beneath. He recognized the outskirt of Eden viewing the approach of the grand walls towering beneath them. Adam was able to pinpoint the location where he first discovered and rescued his partner and mate. Adam and his partner were transported and carried over the wall effortlessly by the gusty winds.

5

The Beginning

The Kingdom fell into complete silence. Not a single creatures dared to speak out or utter a breath to challenge the king's decision. Tree was highly upset and overcome with a range of negative emotions. She believed her master had reacted irrationally in his final judgment of Adam and his companion. Tree was unable to muster the voice to express her feelings openly without fearing retaliation. The intensity of warring emotions provoked Tree to give out a heart-wrenching outcry. "But why?" Tree sobbed woefully before her master. The king felt little remorse however became inwardly distraught and irritated at hearing Tree's out pouring. God did not turn to face Tree, nor would he respond to her outburst. Instead, God remained stoically silent entranced in state of analysis and deep thought. The grave look of concern drawn on the king's face called into question the possible self-examination to his rashness. God struggled with his conscious feeling somewhat torn by his harsh judgment and sentencing. The severity of the punishment now seemed unjust and impulsive in the eyes of the king, qualifying possibly as a blatant abuse and misuse his omnipotence.

The king's temper and nerves began to slowly subside, "Oh well," God reassured himself; growing less tense and annoyed in his reproach to Adam's unwillingness to yield. "In hindsight what seemed like a crisis could have been so easily averted," Tree was scolding herself for not speaking out when afforded the opportunity. She was upset by the circumstantial outcome and more so annoyed by the king's pathology. Tree disagreed entirely with the king's decision and resolution to the matter. Growing more irritated in her temperament Tree struggled to conceal her frustration. She managed to overcome her fears shedding the paralyzing fear of retaliation that was sure to ensue. Tree was now prepared to confront her master and face the wrath and storm of her unjust king. "You have just sentenced them to death." Tree cried out unapologetically livid. She was prepared to embrace the fiery backlash and fury of her master's anguish. "You have wrongly condemned Adam for discovering the most precious and natural quality embedded within him, love..."

"But he was supposed to love me!" God interrupted sharply, looking away off into the distance as he spoke. Tree was humbled by the sincerity of her master's tone and could see first-hand through empathetic lenses that God was troubled and somewhat bothered by his impulsive decision and reaction. Tree considered for a moment the overwhelming burden of emotions that her king harbored in carrying out the dreadful act. "But how could he love you?" Tree posed the question, "when you were never active or present in his life." Tree paused to re-examine her approach feeling the need to offer her objective observations. "My lord, please do not receive my words with malice as it is not my goal or intent to offend my master. However, I feel that my nature and assignment as Adam's guardian and caregiver allows me the dutiful right and obligation to speak openly on the sensitive matter before us." Gods turned about slowly to face Tree still unsure how to respond to her candid solicitation.

Tree was teetering the narrow lines of insubordination and attempted to steer cautiously within the framework of her boundaries. She feared that her honesty in the matter would be seen as an overstep drawing closer to forefront of treason. Surprisingly God did not respond harshly offering little if any reaction at all. Tree accepted the passive and silence of the king as safe passage and vindication to further her exploration.

"I have cared for Adam since childhood watching his growth and ascension to adulthood. I have seen first-hand the sad look of yearning and desperation he often wore behind his smile. His endless search of belonging festered into feelings of hopelessness, and bitter remorse. Adam was young when he began harboring resentment and jealousy towards his friends. He eventually began to isolate himself from those that subscribed to the sacred trinity of family. Adam grew resentful of the children who maintained a unified bond with their creators. When I first noticed this behavior I asked Adam, "why won't you go and play with the other creatures? He responded that the children were mean and teased him often, referring to him as a trail baby. Apparently, the deregulatory term refers to those creatures unworthy of renewal; bastards without fathers." God appeared flustered, his face flush with tension and anguish at the maltreatment of his son by the animals and creatures of Eden. "I remember the day," Tree mourned, "when Adam collapsed before me wallowing and crying out painfully, "why has my father not come for me?" He poured out to me pleading and begging for an answer, but I could not offer him an explanation outside of the superficial."

"I tried my best to sooth his young heart and mend him of his troubles and worries. I offered him words of affirmation and encouragement to restore his sense of pride. It gave him great comfort as child whenever I shared fanciful tales of your amazing feats and contributions. I attempted to secure his pardon and forgiveness for your delayed return and extended absence as best as I could. I provided Adam an extensive collection of appeals and excuses regarding your whereabouts. Whenever the subject of your absence was brought into question, I pacified Adam religiously that you would return for him soon. But as time went on you never returned to claim him. I cannot recall a single instance of you showing up to check on your self-proclaimed precious creation and child. I implore you to accept accountability for your neglect in the matter. For had you maintained communication or allowed for a private meet with Adam during his years of adolescence. His leery mind would have been pacified by the interaction laying to rest the lingering notion that his creator had somehow forsaken him."

The pure honesty of Tree's words stuck a chord that penetrated deep within the heart of its intended target. God felt somewhat fluxed at the same time bewildered and moved by Trees perceptive inclination and encumbering proclivity to truth. Tree's delivery, and transparency was mildly upsetting ,very much so that not even God could deny or dispute the legitimacy of her sounding words. God smiled inwardly amused by the objective power and influence of unbiased truth. He did not interrupt Tree or speak against her actions but stood patiently listening as she expressed her views.

The more Tree defended Adam the more God appeared to grow attentive and receptive to her pleas. He began to better understand and consider how his absence may have contributed to the downward spiral, and degradation of his fondest creation. Tree's love and admiration for Adam was apparent as she spoke with overwhelming compassion in advocacy of Adams defense. Her thoughts were clear and precise as she went on uninterrupted by her king. God stood before Tree like a student listening attentively before the counsel of a somewhat wise and discerning advisor. He slowly began to accept his portion of responsibility in the outcome and turnout of his creation. God recorded these mishaps and errors in his mind to serve as a reference for unseen future endeavors. He waited patiently for the perfect moment and opportunity to respond to Tree, as he had no intention of disrupting the wise instructor. Tree points were valid however she was beginning to drift into an emotional tangent.

"Tree, you are correct." God interjected no longer able to contain his patience, "You have help me to understand that I neglected my obligations to my greatest creation. Had I been active and present to keep watch over Adam, I could have prevented this loathsome outcome, but instead..." God paused overcome with deep emotions "I have managed to spark and ignite a fiery feud between father and son." God dropped his head and gripped the bridge of his nose demonstrating his frustration and tension in the moment. "I assure you Tree" God declared, "in due time Adam will make amends, and I will have my son back." Tree was unsure how to digest her kings' words however drew excitement at the possibility and mention of Adams redemption. Tree understood very well the unfavorable circumstances of Adam's present circumstances. She imagined Adam and his companion wandering aimlessly through the desolate unknowns without access to basic foods or provisioning. Tree pictured a tragic and fatal outcome for Adam and his mate. She imagined seeing their shriveled bodies lying feeble and pruned like raisins beneath the scorching sun.

"No!" Tree interrupted in a defiant uproar, "I cannot live with the thought of Adam being stranded alone outside the perimeters of the grand walls. Outside of Eden he is susceptible to the wildlings and savage predators and beasts. I plea that you grant my request to be placed outside of the grand walls with Adam. I wish to serve as a source of nutrition for Adam helping to sustain and endure through the uncertain rough times ahead. I am confident that Adam will do just as you have prescribed. He will call out for your mercy and plead for your forgiveness and penance through prayer. Just as I am sure that whenever this day arrives you will accept his apology and offer him pardon and clemency for his transgressions." God listened patiently to Tree and considered the hefty weight of her request. The gesture was moving, however in his mind he had already decided the fate of the matter but did not stop or discourage Tree from her cause. "It is to you my lord that I owe my allegiance" Tree reminded her king "but it is through Adam that I have transcended my purpose and meaning of my life and existence."

"I suppose that you are right," God admitted acknowledging Tree's views and overall commitment to the preservation of man. "Seeing as Adam's life and your life have become so intertwined and enmeshed; I have no other choice but to allow you to remain as his guardian and keeper." "Yes!" Tree rejoiced openly expressing her gratitude thanking the kings for his decision, "Thank you your highness, Tree expressed her gratitude repeatedly, "I will continue to nurture and look after Adam until the day of your reunion and reconciliation." Tree considered the historical patterns of her king's behavior foreseeing a long and extended absence, believing it would be some time before God would return for his creation again.

"No!" declared God defiantly dismissing the very notion and thought. "This time Adam will come to me." Tree looked at the king with confusion, "what do you mean?" she asked, but the king did not answer directly. "He must come to me and pray before my feet." "But how can you be so sure that he will return," Tree inquired, "when he has been gifted with free will to make his own choices." "Hmmm," God pondered giving considerable thought to Adam's ability to govern and direct of his will. "I cannot say until I devise a plan which will guarantee Adam's successful return." Tree did not know any other way to aid her grieving king other than to stand at his side in silent mourning. "Are you ready?" God asked Tree somewhat unwillingly, "to be transported to the other side. Tree took a moment to look around over the surrounding garden for the last time. She took in the bounty of beauty and magnificence drawn throughout the lands. She thought of the many friends and neighboring creatures who she would no longer see or receive visits. The toll of her provisional request appeared emotionally taxing and burdensome to endure. Tree accepted her decision with clear uncertainty as to the outcome and future of her fate. "Are you ready?" God repeated once again offering Tree a final opportunity to recant and reconsider her request. "Yes. I am ready." Tree answered finally.

The king did not speak instead he cast his gaze over Tree and raised his finger and waved it vertically. Tree was nervous as she had never been uprooted from her lifelong station. It was the first time Tree would experience such heights, soaring high above the sky like her feathered friends. Tree felt as if she was being rewarded, fulfilling her deepest desire of somehow soaring through the air. Tree had never seen Eden from such an elevated view and vantage point. She soared through the sky marveling over the many beautiful landscapes that decorated her home. Into the distance she observed the ginormous grand wall that Adam had vividly described as stretching far beyond the horizon's peak.

God transported Tree outside of Eden gently stationing her near the base of the towering wall. The location of the stony barrier would assist to provide Tree with shade for part of the day as a means of escape from the sweltering sun. Tree was shocked and surprisingly amazed to find herself overlooking the desolate and barren wasteland. A tingling sensation of joy and excitement overcame Tree like an artist staring over a blank canvas. She understood very well that she was being placed outside of Eden to watch over Adam but observing the barren land she now felt a compelling innate sense to improve the land. The strange calling was no easy feat and would require an unprecedented amount energy and time.

"Thank you, Tree, for your support," God offered his gratitude, "It seems once again you have managed to help aide me in my time of difficulty. Rest reassured that I will not forsake or leave you to fester and whither in this dry barren field." Tree was moved and touched by her kings offer and display of concern. "If ever you wish to abandon this honorable quest and return home. Pray to me and I will bring you back to Eden where you belong." But before Tree could respond, they were interrupted by the groans of Adam and his mate slowly awakening from their arrested state. "Anyhow, good luck to you Tree, "do not hesitate to reach out when necessary." God quickly adjourned their meeting, vanishing suddenly in his usual fashion.

The couple began to awaken from their restful slumber, and quickly rejoiced upon seeing Tree. Unable to contain their excitement they quickly ran to embrace their tender friend. It was obvious to see that Adam and his mate truly loved and cared for Tree a great deal. "But how?" Adam questioned "I thought we left you back in Eden..."

He stopped himself suddenly unable to further thoughts overcome with swelling feelings of guilt and shame surrounding Trees removal. Adam apologized to Tree, offering his condolences for her present circumstances. He assumed that his association with Tree had somehow managed caused her to be disbarred. Nevertheless, Tree's sudden appearance was a cause for great joy and celebration for Adam and his companion as they rejoiced in their reunion.

Tree would later share the story which led to her current placement and disclosed the conditions and terms of Adam's return. "I will never offer him an apology," Adam cursed the thought. "If anything, he should apologize to me." Tree attempted to calm Adam, but her words failed. "Look what God has done to us," declared Adam pulling his mate to his side, "God, has removed my companion's ability to communicate and speak." A loud thunderclap erupted from the sky. The booming sound instantly paralyzed the three momentarily instilling terror and fear. No one spoke for some time with everyone looking around, surveying the area and canvas of their new home. It was easy to observe the depth and vastness of the vacant land. The scattered clouds above their heads began to corral and form into dense fog over the weathering sky. The sudden splash and the pitter patter of raindrops began to fall from the puffy gray sky.

"More rain!" shouted Adam in frustration, "have we not endured enough of his wretched showers." The couple took refuge under the remaining branches of Trees large leafy limbs. "It will take me some time to fully restore my missing limbs and begin my endeavor to make this space into a miniature paradise." The raindrops did not slow down, but instead began to gain momentum. The couple were instantly startled as small pellets of frozen raindrops began hail down over them from the sky. The small rocks and fragments pierced through the air colliding against the dense floor. Standing near the wall the couple could hear pieces of ice crashing hard against the wall behind them. The icy fragments exploded upon impact sending shards of icy debris flying into the air. The pieces of tiny shards pierced and stung the delicate flesh of the exposed couple as they squirmed and shuffled in effort to avoid the sharp painful tacks of the ice rain. Tree cursed her missing limbs for not being able to provide adequate coverage to the troubled couple. Icy droplets penetrated through her branches cutting past her leaves landing painfully against the top and lower parts of Adam and his mate's body. Troubled by the thought of their suffering, Tree would once again provide guidance and encouragement to the tearful couple, "You two must go out and find a place of refuge and shelter to escape this raging storm."

The storm grew more intense with hail pouring down over them. The couple searched and surveyed the uncharted area for a place to take refuge but found only the rocky mountainside far-off in the distance. "We must go," said Adam "We must make our way to safer ground and escape from the piercing skies." "Do not go too far off." Tree called out to the pair as they sped across the rough prickling ground. They ran onward covering their heads from the shower of icy rain beating hard across their shoulders and backs.

The frightened couple seemed perplexed and irritated in their fall and descent from grace. The transition from the flowery wonderland of Eden to the bedrock and stony landscape seemed rather unfavorable. The new environment made entirely of dried clay and dirt would become their new world. The couple raced onward running frantically past the point of exhaustion. Their chest pounded like hard drums running aimlessly across the strange land. Adam grew concerned that their frantic pace would cause his mate fatigue and suggested that they stop to catch their breath. "We should stop and gather some air," Adam suggested panting profusely over his mate. "You are in no condition to continue this run.

His partner declined the suggestion and responded by pointing forward indicating that they should carry on. Adam ignored the feeling of soreness that ached in his legs running closely beside his mate. A breath of salvation came as the two discovered a gaping hole near the mountainside far off into the distance. "Look ahead," Adam encouraged his mate, "we are nearly there. We can make it." The poor creature struggled to keep pace with Adam's holding onto the sizable belly that made running more difficult. Very soon Adam's mate was overcome by fatigue and exhaustion and dropped suddenly onto the floor.

Adam who was a few steps ahead stopped immediately and returned to revive his mate. "You must get up my love" but the creature did not stir or rise. Adam shielded his mate from the elements covering the creature's body with his own. Adam endured the harsh stings from the hail of icy rocks striking hard against his back. Without a moment to waste, Adam delicately scooped his mate into his arms and raised the creature up from the ground. Adam trailed onward keeping a slow but steady pace towards the mountainside. He endured the hailing pang of slapping rain that beat against his face and body. Adam was forced occasionally to stop and press his face between his partners neck and chest just to protect himself from the hailing storm.

Adam fled toward the direction of the large mountain, walking on with cramped and aching legs. He wobbled onward until finally they arrived at an opening in the mountainside. Left with little time to assess the area Adam quickly entered the cave to escape from the abusive climate. Adam gently placed his mate down on the warm dry earth. "We can rest now." Adam encouraged his partner, however the creature was opposed the suggestion and sat up to embrace Adam, holding him close and gripping him tenderly.

Wrapped in each other's arms the couple stood as one shadowy figure before the entranceway. They watched as the shower of icy rain poured down from above. The couple sat together in amazement reflecting over the occurrences of that day. Adam and his mate sat silently holding one another embracing the warmth and heat of their bodies. Together they listened to the acoustic sounds of hailing rain playing sad notes. Adam and his mate sat together watching for a long time as the turbulent storm began to slowly recede and settle down. The gray skies began to break and give way to sunshine and sunlight.

The provisional rays of the sun served as a torch helping to light and illuminate parts of the cavern. Adam and his mate searched around the cave, exploring their new surroundings with the prospect that this would become their new home.

The couple took notice to the sizable den and gave some consideration to the endless possibilities. The cavern was warm and lofty with inaccessibly raised ceilings. It was agreed that the cave would serve as a comfortably dry shelter and dwelling for the couple. The very thought of having secured a new home was enough for the couple to accept the cavern as their permanent residence. Their new residence could never measure up in comparison to the luxuries afforded to them in their previous dwelling. Unlike the garden which provided them a scenic landscape of shrubbery and real estate, their current scenery retained the opposite effect of dreariness. "It is no grand paradise like that of the Eden" Adam proclaimed, "but we are safe here, and can live as we choose within the confines of these hollowed walls."

Adam rejoiced at the noticeable turn of good fortune after locating a safe place and reuniting with Tree their faithful friend and loyal companion. "In the morning, we will go off to see Tree and consult further with her. I am sure that she will provide us with nutritional support, and sustenance as well as provide us with guidance on how to best proceed." The support and company of his beloved friend, and family, leveraged somewhat against the bleak uncertainty of the uncharted wilderness. Adam began to diminish and dispel the frightening sense of destitute hopelessness that lingered within.

The strange new world intrigued the couple, looking over the vastness of the land. They considered the endless possibilities and explorations that would eventually be pursued. Adam was beginning to feel a sense of relief despite the contentious encounter and confrontation with his father. Adam perched his back against the cavern wall with his loving mate resting soundly on his lap. Adam seemed to be at peace preparing himself mentally to brave and explore this new and uncharted world. Despite the despairing reality of his present circumstances, Adam did not feel defeated but reserved an optimistic, and hopeful outlook on their survival and future outside of Eden.

6

The Reasoning

After some time, and adjustments Adam and his mate learned to make the most of their new life. The couple transformed the empty cavern into a cozy dwelling and home rather quickly. Naturally as the seasons passed so did the womb of his companion and mate grow larger, and more engorged in size. The once slender waistline of his partner was now obliquely enlarged and protruded outward. The expecting day was drawing closer for Adams partner to give birth to their offspring. The unborn infant was viewed as the cause of strife and misery over its host.

The active fetus frequently tossed, and turned, kicked and punched while inside the creature's womb. The unintentional abuse went on for some time, leading up to the day of delivery and labor. The birthing process was an uncomfortable and agonizing experience for Adam to bear witness, however the experience rewarded him with a polished layer of respect, and admiration for his partner. Adam was present and witnessed first-hand the daunting task and miracle of childbirth carried out with immeasurable pain and suffering. Adam was saddened and felt sympathy for his mate witnessing the creature in such a distressing condition and state. Many times, Adam felt over-whelmed; tormented internally by the arresting emotions of fear and uncertainty. These malignant feeling of remorse would often emerge as a direct result of Adam's of self-loathing. He nursed grave insecurities about the prosperity and future of his new family. Left unchecked these feelings helped to illicit negative emotions of self-pity, shame, and guilt all which Adam struggled daily to overcome.

Adam felt somewhat responsible for his mate's present condition and state of suffering. The painful sacrifice of childbearing was no simple feat; mostly excruciating. However, the process was necessary to elevate the course and trajectory of their relationship. The addition of a child signified the couples rightful ascension and union in creating and forming a singular being. Adam viewed the dynamic shift as a monumental milestone signifying their passage and indoctrination into adulthood. Adam and his partner had grown accustomed to lavish lifestyle afforded to them in the garden, and initially rejoiced at the thought of welcoming new life. The pair never fathomed the prospect of having to rear their offspring in an unfertile and barren wasteland and environment. Adam in moments of grief paused to consider the notion that their child would be the first creature of its kind to be conceived outside of Eden. He managed to find a thread of hope and drew an optimistic outlook and perspective over the dire scenario. Adam reserved a gleam of excitement at charting his own course and path in life entirely independent of his father influence and affluence. These ideals often stirred inner conflict in Adam whenever confronted by the sight of his distressed and ailing companion confined to a piteous state. It was Adam's personal belief that no creature deserved to endure such grueling pain. The unease and painful discomfort experienced by his mate appeared intentionally deliberate to discourage the act of childbearing. Adam often felt remorseful for the pain which he unintentionally helped to inflict over his partner in the process. He felt overly sentimental and saddened at the fact he could do nothing to alleviate his partners discomfort and pain. Adam wished if nothing more than the ability to ease the agony and numb the soreness of his companions agonizing pain and suffering. Adam would have happily accepted his partners physical pain and discomfort in exchange for the emotional turmoil, and torment he privately faced.

Adam harbored insecurities, and uncertainties about the future, however he nurtured his mate as best as he could. He was affronted on numerous occasions for his lack of consideration and was regularly accused of being insensitive. Adam was often reminded of his helplessness whenever the intense pains of discomfort formed into unbearable outcries. "If only my beloved could speak to me," Adam thought, "then surely I would be able to help and assist in some way." In any case Adam endured the challenge, providing ongoing support to his mate throughout the day, with ongoings services continuing through the night.

One day while at home, Adam found himself overwhelmed and unable stand the incessant feeling of helpless. He appeared rather irritated and annoyed by the impregnable sound of his mates' weeping outcries. Adam decided it best to leave the den to clear his mind and gather fresh air. He left his dwelling with the intention of securing food and nourishment for his mate and unborn child while on his stroll. The sultry sun and humidity caused Adam to sweat out profusely. This rapid loss of water was somewhat alarming as the fear of dehydration was a grave concern living on dried earth. Unlike Eden with its many rivers the dry world reserved a single river stretching several yards from his cavern home. Adam set out daily as part of his routine to procure water and replenishments for his mate and himself. Adam rather enjoyed the task and often used the courier opportunity as an outlet providing him a temporary escape from wailing outcries and painful moans he endured at home. He was tormented by the frightening sounds of sporadic screaming and shouting that occurred without notice or warning.

On his search for nourishments Adam would on many days stop to speak with Tree. Adam rather enjoyed meeting with his guardian and mentor relishing the fluidity of their interaction and engagement. His visits to Tree were oftentimes brief however impactful in keeping him focused and centered. Tree held a multidisciplinary role in Adam eyes wearing many hats, and positions. Tree was a matriarchal guide and guru, mentor, as well as Adams therapist. He provided frequent updates to Tree reporting on the status and condition his mate. Adam often shared his thoughts speaking openly about his emotions and feelings with Tree. She once again settled into the role as being his loyal friend and confidant. Adam greeted Tree as he usually did, taking his regular place and seating by her side. He paid attention to the developing flower patch of grass which Tree was attempting to cultivate.

"Your garden is growing quite wonderfully." Adam would often share his compliments. "Oh why, thank you," Tree would causally reply. "The ground beneath is so coarse and thick," Tree complained, "it is taking me much longer than I anticipated to sprout or grow a simple dandelion from this dry unforsaken earth." Tree laughed out at the sudden thought, "You know Adam, had this been Eden, I would have been growing dandelions and flowers left and right." Adam fell into silence, feeling somewhat remorseful for Tree's current circumstance and the events that had taken place which placed them all here.

Tree observed the withdrawn look of sadness on Adam face and inquired, "What is the matter, Adam?" Adam was reluctant to respond, and almost offered a passive reply. "Nothing, I guess." "You guess," Tree questioned wittingly, "well some would say that guessing is done in the absence of faith." Adam did not wish to be lectured on the principals of faith and spirituality on this day. He corrected himself and offered a clearer more objective response. "I am struggling with the thought that I have made a dire mistake. I fear I have erred in choosing to master my own fate. This life that I live, has become much too complicated." Tree did not respond but allowed allow to complete his thought, and emotionally express the source of his troubles.

"A great sense of helpless has befallen me," Adam sighed, "It is distressing for me to watch my beloved mate suffering with no clear way to express or communicate these pains. My mate has been become non-verbal and unable of speak out or vocalize immediate needs. This cruel and patronizing disability has invited grief and sadness into our home. The punishment serves as a tokened reminder of my offense and act of hubris." Adam began to sob emotionally, "The experience of childbearing is far too hefty a burden for anyone to bare, let alone endure silently. These unforeseen challenges have been taxing on my mind and body. The fee and sum of one's appraisal should not come at the expense and degradation of their soul." Many times, Adam expressed his concerns poetically cryptic and unclear to Tree, while other times he spoke direct and candidly about his feelings. Tree was obliged to provide a supportive and listening ear to Adam, offering regular consult to address his grief and gripes.

Tree exercised patience with Adam choosing to remain silent to allow him to unload his emotional baggage and burdens. Adam safely unpacked his concerns and explored the contents with Tree for subjective processing. Tree understood her role and many times practiced a guiding technique of just listening while probing gently. Tree only offered her thoughts when asked or called upon to offer her sound wisdom and advice. "Do not worry yourself," Tree affirmed Adam in a calming tone, "false expectations can often appear real. The time draws near and very soon the burden of pain and suffering will come to an end. Until that day comes, I pray that you remain diligent in your efforts and continue to sustain and thrive. Please, do not forget who you are, or all that you have sacrificed on your journey. You are powerful beyond belief; fearless and strong. I look forward to the day when you and your child finally meet."

Tree's advice and wisdom set over Adam like soft blanket providing him with a sense of ease and calm. Her assurances helped to wash away and remove the stain of fear and doubt that soiled his mind. Adam accepted Tree's explanation believing that this difficult moment would soon pass. He was overwhelmed with exhaustion and wished for nothing more than for the experience to come to an end. Adam was impatient and yearned deeply to know when the exact day would arrive. He managed the contain the immediate temptation to probe and pursue the subject further which reflected his sense of maturity and personal growth. However, the fleeting moment was short lived as Adam quickly reverted once again to childhood behavior. He felt compelled by his nagging impulse to test the range of his limits and boundaries "But Tree," Adam cried in a whinny tone. "Three seasons have come and passed already. How much longer must I wait, and I suffer the blaring cries of my mate."

Tree was highly offended and irritated by Adam's remark. "Mind your manners," Tree snapped fiercely in a condemning tone, "You are short sighted if you cannot see that your mate is the one who suffers most. You should be at your partners side, not here frolicking with me." Her words stung like a blister against Adams frail and fragile ego. Tree seemed rather annoyed and upset by Adam's insensitivity and lack of empathy to the matter. It was becoming embarrassingly blatant to Adam, observing by Tree's response that he had somehow crossed an unfamiliar line and boundary. In his heart and mind Adam knew that Tree's honest words were irrefutable facts, however he questioned the method and tact of her delivery. Hearing these truths uttered out loud was a painfully jarring experience for Adam. The bitter mixture of truth and reality produced a potent elixir that was far too strong for Adam to ingest. Tree's temper though unpleasant appeared to be the correct response to Adams demonstration of insensitivity. Her chastising remarks served as the appropriate prescription and treatment to tame and check Adam's ego and correct his behavior.

"Go, now," Tree continued, "go to your mate, and be at your partners side, I am not your refuge, nor am I a means of escape from your troubles." Adam was stunned with confusion, and disbelief. He did not understand how a simple inquiry could warrant such levels of mistreatment of unkindness. Adam did not budge and instead looked on in dazed confusion at his annoyed matron. "Go away Adam!" Tree demanded, "aide your mate and unborn child, for if you forsake the poor creature, then two lives will surely perish. Go home my dear Adam and return only after your mate has birthed your child."

Adam was disturbed by the unfamiliar bulk of Tree's flaring demeanor. No further words were spoken between the two with Adam appearing annoyed that his feelings and ego had been somehow bruised by the unprovoked confrontation. He abated Tree's crudeness, and in silence began to depart. Adam walked away without the thought of looking behind him. Had he taken the opportunity to look back Adam would have found the tearful face of his dearest friend. Her intense and seemingly fierce eyes were now moist and dampened against the brownness of her bark and skin. Adam returned home bearing the needed replenishments, still feeling rather annoyed by the earlier encounter with Tree. Adam decided right then that he would learn to master the domesticated life assigned to him. He vowed to become the greatest version of himself, and in doing so managed to channel his pain and frustration into useful productive energy. Though spitefully committed to the goal of achieving independence and autonomy his motivation posed certain benefits. Adam began to adopt an entirely new outlook and mindset tailored around increasing personal development and self-improvement.

Over time Adam began to increase his resilience growing very much accustomed to the sounds and noises produced by his mate. He became less anxious to the sudden and sporadic outcries of his partner. He seemed to no longer be affected by the wounding shrieks and screams of his delicate partner. The alarming sounds no longer pestered or irritated Adam as it had before. Adam developed an immunity to the painful moans and groans of his fragile mate by way of endurance and repeated exposure. The newly adopted mindset appeared to benefit Adam making him emotionally impervious to outside disturbances and irritations. He developed a heightened sense of patience and humility as part of his character. Adam began to exercise self-discipline and practice self-restraint over his actions and impulses. He changed his perception and now viewed his mates' cries as indication that their unborn child still thrived and was apparently eager to meet them.

Adam attended to the needs and care of his mate prioritizing comfort and support. He made all the proper accommodation to ensure that his mate was comfortable and well at ease. He would often rub his partners sore and swollen feet and massage the creatures aching back. When offered the opportunity Adam would place his hands over his mates, inflated belly to feel the kicks and jerks of their unborn child. "Our child is restless," Adam laughed out loud to his partner, "such an active and anxious creature quite eager to make its long-awaited debut." He caressed his companion's tummy and spoke directly to the creature's belly. "From the womb to the world." Adam joked playfully. His mate offered him a smile that indicated amusement at Adams playful and silly behavior. Adam managed to find his happiness sitting at home in the company of his family.

7

The Delivery

One hot day as Adam was returning home from an afternoon of gathering food, he heard a loud wailing cry coming from the direction of his home. The dreary moans of his mate echoed through the cavern walls before escaping into the open air. The loud distant cry of his mate immediately drew Adams attention and seized his nerves quickly before filling him with fright and terror. Adam imagined his mate to be in a state of distress, and immediately began to sprint and race home. The painful outcry was an intense sound that rung through the air followed shortly by howling screams and loud shrieks.

The passage of alarming noises pushed Adam to move even quicker, as he hastened his pace shifting his sprint and extending his stride a great distance. The sack of food that slung over his shoulders began to spill onto the floor colliding against his backside. Adam was concerned at the very moment by the loss and sprang like a mustang charging towards his home. It seemed the faster he ran the louder the screams echoed. He sprinted like a cheetah in chase of game, moving swift and agile as the wind. His feet beat repeatedly against the ground causing discomfort and pain. Adam ran as though he was competing in an exhibition facing an imaginary clock. The dense humidity of the dry land only helped to increase the temperature of the already hot and sultry air. Adam seemed unfazed in his pursuit ignoring the sharp aches and soreness in his legs and joints. He was relentless in his pursuit determined to reach home in time to aide and assist his mate. Adam endured unbearable pain which throbbed and ached through his body pulsating from the soles of his sore feet to the bridge of his shoulders.

Adam arrived at the entranceway of the cavern and barged into the den searching wildly around his home for an intruder or trespasser. The air drew strangely silent, the loud screams had suddenly ended. Adam moved quietly through the long corridor and passageway into his home. Stepping delicately Adam was immediately gripped with the dreadful thought and fear that he had somehow arrived too late. A loud scream sprang suddenly from deep within the bowels of the unlit and shadowy cave. The terrifying scream startled Adam causing him to retreat quickly back outside in reaction to the frightening noise.

Adam stood outside the entranceway of the cave paralyzed in fear. The confidence and momentum he collected during his sprint had suddenly vanished. Lost possibly amongst the assortment of foods that he dropped during his climatic sprint. Adam wanted to enter the cavern but found himself frozen with terror crippled somewhat by the deafening screams echoing deep within dim cavern walls. Adam slowly overcame his fears and reservations beckoned by the call and need to act on behalf his beloved partner and mate. He peered into the dark cave assessing much of the shadowy room before slowly inching back into the gloomy cave.

Adam once again found himself walking timidly back though the entranceway and corridor of his home. He managed somehow to move his quivering legs guided solely by doubt and uncertainty with every step. A sudden loud outcry filled the air, the painful sound echoed loudly off the walls. Adam was instantly alarmed and jumped back quickly plastering his body against the cavern wall. He was once again gripped by fear and began panting nervously to sooth his pounding chest. Adam was prepared if not ready to take flight at any moment demonstrating a sense of hyper vigilance to any sudden signs of impeding danger.

The circumstances at hand revealed a truth that Adam often repressed and hid from himself. Adam was secretly frightened if not terrified of the very moment and event which he had been anticipating. In his mind he found himself considering the thought of turning back and fleeing. He began to fantasize the unknown possibilities of living out the rest of his days carefree in wanton freedom. But somehow the thought of absconding and scurrying away seemed like a cowardly route and path. The intrusive daydream that invaded Adams imagination was short lived, quickly derailed by a dreary afterthought. Adam began to view dismal images portraying an unfortunate outcome.

Adam imagined quite vividly the effect and outcome of the selfish decision to flee. He saw the body of his mate lying lifeless on the cavern floor. The brittle body and frame of his partner hunched against the cavern walls appeared lifeless. Tucked between the cold arms of his mate was a small fragile creature that Adam took to be their newborn. The infant creature's small body was feeble, and helplessly malnourished. The newborns face appeared faint and was absent of both vigor and life. The creature looked sickly and ill rapidly approaching the brinks of death. Adam collapsed into a sea of drenching tears after viewing the sight and image of his family in such a despairing and fatal state. Adam was instantly overcome with guilt and shame for having ever entertained the thought and idea of abandoning his family.

This dramatic revelation had an impactful effect over Adam. He shunned the heinous thought of fleeing and leaving his family behind. He slowly began to rebuild his confidence and sought desperately to regain control of his nerves. Adam's heart thumped rapidly beneath his chest as he attempted to tame the racing thoughts of his odd imagination. The lucid daydream would have continued longer had it not been for the sudden and sharp yell from his mate which quickly jogged Adam from his lucid daydream. He was brought to the sudden realization that his mate was in labor and was preparing to give birth at any moment. Adam refused to allow for his mate to endure the frightening experience alone. He could hear Tree's voice echoing in the back of his mind, warning him to look after his partner, "if you forsake the poor creature then two lives will surely perish." Adam reacted quickly scurrying through the dim cavern in search of his mate. He discovered his companion perched helplessly against the cave wall. The grave image resembled the fatal scene he conjured just moments before. Adam drew a sigh of relief rejoicing after discovering that his partner and mate very much alive, just barely. His mate perspired profusely and appeared fever stricken with quivering starchy lips. Adam sought to aide his mate and moved quickly to be at his partner's side. "Are you parched," He inquired holding his mate in his arms. The creature nodded agreeably causing beads of sweat to trickle and run down his partners moist face.

Adam scurried frantically though the cavern in search of a pitcher to carry water to his mate. He raced back and forth darting clumsily about in search of a potted container. Adam managed to locate the large vase like object that held and stored their water rations. His nerves and hands quaked nervously while attempting to draw water from the vase container into the pitcher. Adam returned to his partner entirely drenched wielding a nearly empty pitcher. His mate quickly clutched the cup of water and drank greedily of the little water that remained. A sharp and sudden pain produced an explosive outcry from his mate. The laboring creature gave out another painful cry and gripped tightly to Adam's arm.

Looking into the tearful eyes of his beloved mate Adam felt as though he was staring directly into the sun. He could no longer bare the blinding light of pain of distress drawn over his partners face. A rush of warm liquid began to trail from between the creature legs. Adam peered down to glance below and nearly jumped back startled after witnessing the cusp and crowning taking place beneath. Adam collected his composure accepting that the blessed moment had finally arrived. Their precious bundle of joy and child would soon be upon them. Adam dropped flat onto his stomach stationing himself between the thighs and legs of his mate.

"I can see it." Adam shouted with growing excitement "It's coming out!" He yelled out to his partner, who was experiencing the intense labor quite differently. The creature screamed and cried out violently while enduring unbearable pains. The couple never imagined or presumed that childbearing would entail such a high degree of pain and discomfort. Adam attempted as best as he could to sooth his mate's agony and pain by offering word of reassurance and encouragement "You can do it," Adam cheered his mate on, "you are almost there, just a little further."

The cavern walls echoed with the indistinguishable sounds of both pain, and excitement. Adams's generous words and encouragement did little to soothe or remove the splintering pains of labor. Adam began weep watching helplessly as his mate struggled relentlessly crying out in painful anguish. It was a rare and vulnerable moment for Adam never having experienced such an intensity of helplessness. Adam felt powerless to ease his mates suffering and pain blaming himself for having placed his companion in touch a compromising predicament and ordeal. However, this was not the right time for self-loathing, and doubt. Adam's mate needed his support as would their child. He understood there was nothing he could do than to keep his mate in good spirits. Adam attempted to uplift his partners spirits with persistent affirmations and sound words of encouragement. Adam evoked the spirit of resiliency and determination while simultaneously retaining the space of an avid spectator enthusiastically chanting on his favorite competitor and athlete to persevere.

The very image could be perceived as laughable with Adam crouched between the legs and thighs of his insufferable mate. He cheered the creature on providing positive affirmations and words of encouragement as his only source of tools. Adams optimism and encouragement was received by his mate and reciprocated with loud painful screams. His partners unbearable wailing appeared intolerable stemming from the bowels of discomfort and pain. A loud deafening scream followed by a final push would bring an end to his mate's distressed state. The burden and weight of childbearing was finally lifted, the daunting labor process was now complete. Adam, and his mate rejoiced after having successfully delivered the first child and newborn into this world.

Adams mate was drained and overcome with fatigue and crippling exhaustion. The creature held its breath and only released a heaving sigh of relief after hearing the newborns cry fill the open air. Adam scooped the newborn infant into his arms and marveled at the creature nestled between his bosoms. "Welcome," Adam greeted the newborn observing the creature's indicator. "Son, we have been waiting for you," he laughed out loudly. The frail creature was not amused by Adam's act of banter and produced a cackling outcry, Adam rejoiced in child's play, finding delight and amusement in the wailing music and song of the newborn infant.

Adam brought the tearful child to rejoin his mother, and gently handed the newborn over to the care of his partner. Almost instinctively the small creature began to quiet down settling into silence. The delicate child was placed across its mother's soft bosoms and was swaddled delicately by the creatures' gentle arms. The tender moment was timeless. This day would forever be ingrained in Adams mind and heart as a definitive hallmark and stapling in his life. The grace and good fortune that now blessed their home would serve as the couple's vindication, propelling them into adulthood. A soothing flow of silence and calm overtook the air filling the home with an abundance of bliss and joy. The tender moment yielded endless possibilities for the newly anointed parents. Adam and his mate were hopeful and optimistic in their outlook of a fortunate and promising future.

Feeling self-absorbed and filled with pride Adam rose slowly on to his feet. He was overcome with a newly rejuvenated with the sense of purpose. He walked delicately through the long corridor of their den stopping at the entranceway of the cave. Looking out yonder staring far off into the distance Adam found himself once again absorbed in deep thought. The world seemed renewed in Adam's eyes.

The air smelled fresher, and the sun shone brighter than usual. Adam thought about traveling to visit Tree to deliver the good news but decided it best to hold off on any expeditions at this current time. Adam celebrated the victory privately in his mind rejoicing gleefully at the thought of his conquest and defiance in bringing forth new life. Adam felt as though he had chosen his own path; a path which his father forbade him to tread. "I will not just be a creator," Adam swore privately, "I will be ten folds the protector and provider that my father and creator was for me." Adam made the commitment and promise to himself, "I will show my creation unconditional love and demonstrate unyielding devotion. I will be active for my creation present to offer wisdom and guidance for the creature's growth and development into greatness."

8

The Fear

Adam stood at the entranceway feeling fatigued however wearing a lighthearted smile. He yielded an immense sense of pride and joy at his triumphant accomplishment. "I do not believe that I will be able to find sleep," Adam shouted from the doorway; his words echoing loudly through the dark cavern. "Not without the blaring sounds of insufferable wailing and screaming." He bantered playfully to his mate but received no sound or noise in response to his ill humor. There was a lingering air of silence that prompted Adam to return and rejoin his family. Adam walked through the cavern in considerably high spirits, he was comforted by the thought of obtaining a peaceful night's rest. Adam felt assured that he would be able to enjoy a peaceful night's sleep now that their child had been successfully delivered. Adam wore an impish grin plastered over his face after securing a full pitcher water to bring to his mate.

Adam's heart dropped suddenly removing the moment of brief joy and excitement. Looking over the body of his fallen mate Adam felt paralyzed and gripped with fear. The sensation of joy and delight diminished quickly before his very eyes. Adam appeared devastated and utterly distraught by the unfortunate outcome. He viewed the exasperated and labile body of his beloved mate slumped against the cavern wall. A sharp pain pierced directly through Adam's heart finding himself deeply afflicted by the unfortunate turn of events. Adam experienced the plight of his hopes and dreams spiraling into a space of bitterness and anguish.

Adam felt heartbroken undoubtedly destroyed by the impact of his descent. The grave sight of his mate resembled the dreary images he fought desperately to shed from his thoughts. Adam could hardly look up to face the lifeless body of his soul mate laying inanimate against the cavern wall. A burst of tears began to pour from Adams eyes flooding the sides of his face. My vision!" Adam whispered audibly, the words narrowly escaping his lips and breathe, "Please, this cannot be true." Adam pleaded mournfully drawing closer to the body of his befallen mate. Adam was bewildered and confused left wondering how his fatal premonition came to fruition.

Adam laid the pitcher of water before the foot of his mate, and slowly placed his arms around the fallen creature. His heavy head hung low weighed by grief and overwhelming pain. Adam cradled the creature in his arms and plunged his face between the chest and shoulders of his lifeless mate and began sobbing uncontrollably. Adam was grief stricken by the current outcome of his circumstances. He accepted the defeating loss of his companion as an omen signifying misfortune to adversity to come. Adam sat disarmed staring off into an endless abyss of nothingness. His hands trembled and shook nervously from the transactional exchange. "A life for a life," Adam reasoned as best as he could trying to make sense of it all. The pain he felt in his heart, could not be quenched by logical reasoning or rational thoughts, "Death is too taxing of a toll," Adam shook his head pleading remorsefully, "to pay for a minor hubris infraction and offense."

Adam was riddled with grief and despair unable to accept or come to terms with the devastating loss. "But why?" Adam cried out woefully "I do not understand what happened, or what went wrong, And what of our child. Wait our child!" Adam recalled soberingly. His eyes darted about searching over and around the body of his mate. Adam searched for the newborn and began to grow increasingly worried after not being able to visually locate the child. Adam immediately dropped to the ground falling onto his knees to conduct a diligent ground search. He used his hands to molest the dampened earth patting the ground around the body of his mate. Adam managed to use his fingers like antennas to feel the ground moving about through blinding darkness.

The terrifying thought of an accidental fatal misstep kept Adam low and grounded to the floor. His fingers nervously combed over the dampened dirt partly fearful of what he may discover awaiting him. The cavern was now pitched and covered in darkness; Adam strained to move his mate's body fearfully uncertain as to which direction to move the stiff body. He hunched himself over the fallen body and wedged his fingers between the creature's body and moist earth. Adam lifted the lammed body of his companion tilting the creature over slightly to allow space for him to search.

Adam discovered on the dampened ground the afterbirth and remains of his partners warm liquids over the moist earth. He cast his eyes around desperately surveying the floor until finally he spotted a protruding object. The small silhouette like creature was covered entirely in dirt and blood. Adams heart dropped into the pits of his stomach. He was suddenly gripped with an overwhelming sense of terror. His eyes began swell with bitter tears absorbed in the anguish and despair. "Mmm..., mm..., my child." Adam stammered to phrase the words which filled him with overwhelming sadness and frustration. "No not your life as well!" Adam grieved the painful thought of having lost two lives on this cursed day. Adam crawled nervously closer to the child. He feared the thought of seeing death drawn on the face and lips of the small infant creature. Adam discovered the small child lodged beneath layers of soft mud and debris. Adam managed to move the dead weight off his partners body from engulfing and smothering their child.

Adam struggled with much difficulty to hold up the body of his mate with one arm, while attempting simultaneously, to pry and extract their child with the other. Adam exercised great physical discipline to maintain the strength and force need hold up his mate while attempting to retrieve their child. With the strenuous weight of his mate barreling down on him Adam was determined more than ever to remove the cold body of his partner off the trapped newborn. Gathering up his strength Adam pushed hard forcing the lifeless body over onto its side. This hurling impact incidentally caused the creature to produce a soft humph sound upon impact.

Adam was instantly startled and jumped back fearfully before realizing that his mate was still very much alive. The exerted creature had succumbed to exhaustion and passed out shortly after giving birth to the newborn. Adam was ecstatic and rejoiced after hearing the soft sounds of his mates' warm breath. Despite the turn of good fortune there was little time to celebrate. Adam moved quickly to save their infant child's life, he dug up the young infant creature and cradled the child in his arms. He handled the fragile infant nervously searching for any indication of life. Adam brought the child closer to his face and listened attentively with heightened senses for a heartbeat. Adam gently caressed the small infant in attempt to provoke a response.

The duration of the entire ordeal may have only lasted a few minutes however the experience would be everlasting. At that very moment holding his child in his arms Adam was not ready to let go. Adam was unwilling to lose the very life he had been entrusted to protect and keep safe. He attempted to revive the child by vigorously rubbing against the infant's sternum and back. Adam massaged the newborn intensely with the tips of his fingers and even resorted to the use of palms.

At the very moment, Adam was fighting for the life and soul of his child. He pleaded out loud repeatedly begging for mercy and praying for the newborn to awaken. "Please God, Please God." Adam unknowingly found himself chanting repeatedly beneath his breath, each time more merciful than the last. He stroked his palm repeatedly across the child's back until finally a loud cry broke suddenly from the small creature's mouth. The infant's outcry was a call for joy and served as a source of relief for Adam. "My child" Adam sobbed pitifully, "you startled me beyond my greatest fears." The small child wailed uncontrollably; each howling scream seem to bring Adam great delight and reason to rejoice.

Adam listened happily to the of sound of his child tearful cries. He rejoiced before the wailing orchestra playing in the background like a symphonic tune. The piercing sound restored Adam's hopes and aspirations at fatherhood. He felt revived and somewhat inspired by the show of resilience demonstrated by the small infant child. "You found your way out," Adam laughed, "just to give me a freight." The small child responded to the sound of Adam's voice with cooing curls and indistinguishable laugher. The rejoicing sounds of echoing laughter helped to stir and awaken his mate. The poor creature slowly began to regain consciousness all but unaware of the wrenching ordeal which had just taken place.

The frightening experience was quite unnerving for Adam at the time. He sat down carefully perching himself beside the coiled frame of his lethargic partner. Adam rejoiced tearfully his face bathed and covered in moist dew. He drew a sigh of relief at the realization that that his family was safe. Adam was eternally grateful somewhat delusional in the extended power of his will and determination. Adam dismissed the transactional belief that he once catered to and harbored. He rejoiced graciously that no exchange of life had taken place, and that their union would remain unsevered. Turning his head over to look at his mate Adam could scarcely make out the face of his partner sitting beside him. His mate leaned in closer to rest comfortably against Adam's shoulders. Despite the absence of light in the room Adam could see with full clarity the soft face and smile that shone on the faces of his mate and child. Adam cradled the infant on his chest with one arm, while comforting his tired and overwhelmingly exhausted mate in the other. The formidable task was no easy feat, somewhat foreshadowing his dutiful obligations as provider and protector of his family and home. Adam summoned his inner strength mustering what little energy remained to hold both his mate and child in his arms. Sitting side to side Adam and his mates faces gently touched as their bodies nestled together in closeness. The picturesque image would forever reign supreme capturing the illustrious and symbolic image of the sacred trinity.

The wild winds blew loudly whistling from outside the cavern into the night. A sudden chill of brisk air was felt slowly entering the dampened cavern. A chilling ominous force disguised as breeze was felt present among their company. Adam felt uneasy by the chilling presence and decided it best to gather his mate, and child and relocate them further into dark den. In one effortless motion Adam swooped and raised his mate and child into his arms. He lifted the pair from the damp ground and moved them to the warmer area of the cave. Adam managed to find a dry location deep within cavern and placed his family down on the ground in full view of the entranceway. He safely secured his mate and child ensuring they were well kept before leaving out to fetch and collect fresh water. Adam returned home shortly bearing water and fresh fish protein which would help to prolong the life and health of his family. Adam prepared a generous meal creating a delicacy of a feast for his mate in honor and celebration of unity and union as a family.

Despite his valiant efforts in preparing a remarkable meal unfortunately his mate would not eat. The sickly creature struggled to mend its appetite and rejected the nourishing meal preferring instead a diet of rest and sleep in substitute of food. Adam did the best he could to sustain his family and comfort the pair. Adam was able to fashion a blanket entirely crafted from leaves and grass. Fastened together with sticky sap and mossy dew Adam was able to form somewhat of an organic quilt. The utilization of sap as adhesive was insightful skill that Adam learned while living inside in the garden. Adam laid down beside his mate and child to rest both his body and mind for the first time in a long time.

The next morning as misfortune would have it Adam woke up to find his mate gravely ill and bedridden. The creatures face gleamed with beads of warm sweat rolling down the moist creatures' body. His companion appeared to be afflicted with a severely crippling fever. His mate would not stir or move from the infirmary of allotted bed space. The creature often refused awaken to eat and would often wage war whenever Adam dared to force feed the malnourished creature. The health rate of his mate began to slowly decline diminishing further with each passing day. Adam tried desperately to offer his assistance and support however soon realized that he could not help his mate alone. The creature had fallen ill flushed with a blazing fever that Adam was unable help or treat.

"Had this been Eden," Adam resented. "I could have easily conjured a remedy from the flowers and leaves of the willow tree but..." A sharp cry broke out into the air that distracted Adam from his thoughts. The shrieking siren managed to startle Adam instantly paralyzing him in his place. The deafening cries continued throughout the night offering Adam little time for a moment rest. The intrusive noise mostly yells and screams became a source of inner turmoil and frustration for Adam. Adam was confused and somewhat unsure as to the cause of his mates ailing troubles especially now that their child was now nowhere near the womb. Adam began to grow more concerned about the health and wellness of his partners as the days went on. He worried helplessly in silence gauging over the intensity and frequency of painful noises produced by his mate.

Adam studied his mates condition becoming quite inept and accustomed to the variations of his partners outcries. He was able to distinguish most of the time with accuracy the extent in which the duration of pain would last by the intensity of his partners aches and screams. Adam would prepare himself and wait for the elusive screams produce randomly like an unsuppressed cough or a random sneeze appearing sporadically without cue. Adam felt a sense of defeat by the incessant noise and wished for nothing more than sooth his mate. He wanted to cure his partner and somehow bring an end to the feverish pain and chilling discomfort experienced was beloved.

9

The Forging

As days passed Adam's perception of the newborn began to grow more perverse, and delusional. Adam was overly exhausted and lacked adequate sleep while caring for his mate and newborn. Adam began to view his newborn not as an innocent defenseless creature, but rather as a parasite content with sucking energy and life force from its host. Adam could only watch with helpless contempt and anguish as the small infant drank greedily from the bosoms of its mother's frail chest.

Adam's eyes often flared with rage watching the dyad in their routine feedings. Adam perceived the child as overindulging with little regard or consideration for the health and welfare of its benefactor. He watched his infant suckle and drank greedily with muse and content. The newborn creature guzzled its meals sucking away at his mother with every churning kiss.

"What sort of creature," Adam questioned "latches itself to the feeble chest of its helpless mother like a leech." The child appeared committed to devouring its host beyond to the brinks of general nourishment. Adam was affected by the current outlook of his present circumstances. The position of an observing bystander did not sit well with Adam who was becoming more irritable, and hostile than usual. He was beginning to gradually change his demeanor and attitude towards the less pleasant and inpatient. The transitional change was strange for Adam outside of his usual character renowned for his love and gentleness. It appeared that the rigid tasks and challenges of adult-hood weighed unfavorably against Adam. He despised the daunting and dutiful role of having to nurse and attend to his ailing mate while simultaneously rearing and caring for their newborn.

Despite the adversity and present challenges Adam stood firm re-fusing to shy away from the newly appointed role. It brought Adam a profound sense of honor in fulfilling his duties as head of his house-hold. Initially, Adam accepted the modest and noble role welcoming the unforeseen challenges of parenthood and was open to the expe-rience. But as time went on Adam would discover that the burden and responsibility of primary caretaker was an overwhelming and un-bearably thankless job. The overhaul of his good intentions was be-ginning to weigh heavily on Adams heart and mind. Most days he was able to ignore and dismiss the symptoms of plaguing emotions which accosted and bombarded his mind and troubling his inner thoughts. Images often appeared to Adam's flickering off and on in the back of his mind. Adam's school of thought had become a campus of resentment of which he resembled an astute alumnus well versed on the subject and curriculum of harbored resentment.

Despite his warring emotions Adam never shied away from an op-portunity to hold the tender newborn. Adam often cradled the boy in his arms and spoke to the small infant as though a creature of equal intelligence. "It must be nice to be pampered and waited on." Adam chastised jovially, "To wake up and hurl your demands, like a prince, no better yet a king upon his throne." Adam mocked playfully at the thought and laughing out loud so mimicked the small infant. The de-fenseless newborn often responded to his creator's sense of humor with reaffirming smiles backed by cooing laughter. Though as triv-ial, and meaningless as the gesture appeared, it was moments like this whenever the child smiled or cooed that the sounds of joyful inno-cence and laughter seemed to disarm and sooth Adam removing ten-sion and anguish from his heart.

The innocent sound of childish laughter garnered the potential to disarm the most explosive and contentious temper. There were times and instances when bouts of anguish would grip and hold Adam like a hostage refusing his release. It was during the height of such tense moments that Adam would breakdown and swear off the daunting assignment and weight of responsibility. However, each time he arrived at the same conclusion viewing walking away and abandoning his post and position as spineless. It was his love for his mate and child which helped to ground Adam, taming his growing impulse and urge to resign and leave from his station.

Adam truly loved and adored his family and was easily subdued by the subtle gaze of his mate's soft eyes and warm touch. The bouncy joyful energy of their newborn often adorned with a large smile help to tame and subdue Adams brooding temper. He was still fearful that the child, would eventually drink his mother past the brinks of death. Adam having expressed this concern to his mate encouraged for the titration and transitioning of liquid to soft foods. Despite Adam's persistence and good intentions on the matter his sound thoughts, and lofty concerns were not well regarded. There were many instances and opportunities when Adam attempted to bring up the sensitive topic of nutrition for discussion, however his futile attempts were often met with stonewalling resistance. The dimming gesture of indifference was the common theme and usual reception that Adam received in response to his wayward proposals. Adam however held firm to his urging convictions of prioritizing wellness and safety.

Adam did not want to see his fears come to fruition and wrestled against the impulse to impose his power and will as sovereign ruler and protector of his home. Adam was precautious, and attentive, his intentions were aimed at avoiding the unnecessary demise and end of his mate and partner. Adam championed his concerns without rhetoric or inquisition and began stating his demands flagrantly in a firm and demanding tone. Adam found himself plunging face first into the role of an authoritative dictator, exercising dominance in his home. Adam in sense placed his foot firmly down into the fertile grounds of intolerance, imposing guidelines and house rules. These cautionary guidelines resembled somewhat lawful doctrines that Adam believed should always be upheld.

One of Adams rules included that there were to be no feedings in their home without him being present, "I want to be near whenever you feed our child, seeing as your fever has yet to subside, it is no doubt that the ailment is still within you." Adam looked into his companion eyes while gently caressing his partners hands. He communicated his gripes and concerns to his mate. "You are not well, my dear." Adam admitted "you must rest and preserve your strength to restore your health, for it is I that needs you the most." Adam's kind words would not betray him, and neither did the gleam of passion that ensued in his eyes. His compassion and commitment to caring for his family did not go unnoticed by his mate. The frail creature though unable to communicate words of gratitude often rewarded Adam regularly demonstrating intimate acts of affection. The common practice of intimacy helped to further their bond and liven their spirits. No ailment or sickness could detour the two lovers from pursuing their basic primal instincts and urges.

His mate could sense the warmth and heat that pulsated through Adams body whenever he laid down to rest. It occurred usually at night that his companion would offer Adam soothing relief from the stress and tension of his worries and troubles. The tender act and practice brought both creatures pleasure, exposing through stolen breaths the natural yearning and irrefutable truth that throbbed within the veins of two beings. There existed within Adam a naturally insatiable hunger and urge to sow his loins. Compelled by the lustful need to procreate Adam would in a sense place his seeds into delicate earth of his companion. The absence of discourse only helped to further the advancement of innocent play before morphing into a seductive and passionate dance between two lovers. In his pursuit of pleasure and fulfillment Adam once again found himself engaged in the euphoric behavior. The pleasurable ascension and practice often helped to raise his lowly spirits to heights of ecstasy and delight.

Adam was growing rather insightful regarding his unrestrained passion, but only after having reached climax. He regained control of his body as well as the lucidity and clarity of his thoughts. He regarded his intense lustful appetite as his only personal flaw and known weakness. Adam was in tune with his body understanding how powerless he was in warding off the sensual feeling that would suddenly eclipse and consume him. In those lecherous and helpless moments Adam often surrendered his will to the prowess power and touch of his enchanting mate. Simply spellbinding, the beautiful dance finally concluded. The symphony of passion that orchestrated triumphantly in their hearts began to slowly die and wither fading softly into the background. The cloud of ecstasy where the couple laid their bodies was a bed of love in which the two took sanctuary and comfort just beneath the realms of paradise. The high spirited coupled began to slowly descend floating delicately back down to the soft fertile earth. Their conclusion marked the end to an outstanding and sensational tune. The masterful body of work scored between the two lovers would stand the test of time as a proven tribute and ode to love.

The passionate act was revitalizing and felt most necessary especially for Adam who struggled with an inner turmoil. He harbored a host of warring emotions mostly feelings of shame and guilt. A sense of remorse and sympathy overcame Adam whenever he considered the grave health and feeble condition of his frail and ailing mate. It pained Adam to acknowledge and come to terms regarding his apparent lack of self-control over of his lustful desires. Adam being critical on himself questioned whether he would ever gain mastery over his perceived flaw. Adam was committed to developing a stronger sense of self-discipline whenever confronted or faced with the yearning sensation and temptation.

These thoughts and more surfaced Adams mind entangling him in deep web of needless thoughts. One night Adam was observed sitting peacefully in silence near the entrance of their home. Looking up at the fluorescent moon glowing brightly over the land, Adam could not help but notice the radiance of light casting down over the barren earth. The bright moon hovered high above the gaping mouth of their cavern home. The strange and somewhat deliberate placement of the moon seemed intentional to allowing for light to refract and extend partially into the passageway of their home. The peaceful moment was nostalgic; reminding Adam of quieter times when he as a child would stay awake at night staring aimlessly into the glowing face of the moon. The night scene was peacefully serene with the gentle winds blowing cool air into their home. Adam reflected on his present circumstance and began to view his current predicament with a lens of optimism. He began to foster a hopeful mindset and outlook believing that their current station was only temporary and that happier more prosperous times would eventually ensue. He began to draw confidence that his family would assimilate successfully and hopefully thrive in the strange new world. Adam stoked and fanned in his mind and heart the hope of rejuvenation. The flicker of hope would soon birth a small flame within Adam, before igniting suddenly into fiery blaze. Adam stood up with excitement eager to share his optimism and positive outlook with his family. However, as he walked over to his mate, he found the two companions sound asleep. His mate was resting comfortably with their newborn clutched between bosom and arms. It appeared that the weary caretaker and newborn both lacked Adam's nocturnal instincts and had long since given into exhaustion.

Adam sat beside his family in silent contemplation, staring helplessly into the face of his beloved mate. Adam could not sleep on this night finding himself in deep yearning of a gentle touch. He reminisced over the preceding events leading to courtship reliving the very moment again in his mind. Adam considered acting on his impulses, however felt conflicted by the swelling urge to sever the tender bond between mother and child. Adam imagined his decision to interrupt the peaceful moment would be met with silent criticism and scolding indifference. Such extremes greatly affected the direction of their interaction often impacting the willingness and participation of mate. Adam seemed to struggle with inner conflict attempting to manage powerful emotions of nagging temptation and lust.

Adam began to view his declaration to self-discipline as unnatural and perversely flawed. The exercise of self-restraint examined Adams character and ability to control his lustful urges. Adam had grown accustomed to the unrestricted access and favorable treatment in which he received from his partner. Typically, Adam's sexual advances went unchallenged, but now times were different, he soon found himself faced with having to justify his cause by way of reasoning and adamant pleading. There were many times, and instances when Adam would become upset and highly irritated reverting somewhat to childish behavior. Whenever denied or faced with rejection Adam would become upset and irritable throwing fits resembling tantrums for the sake of his cause. Adam's petitions were usually met with opposition and defiance however, being head strong and persistent he managed to negotiate the eventual submission of his partner pinned by shame and guilt. It did not help that his mate was unable to communicate or speak out against Adam deplorable conduct and behavior. The routine practice of courtship had become a difficult labyrinth for the couple to tread and navigate. The sensual practice of relations began to subside occurring less frequently for the staled lovers. Adam and his mate were beginning to forget the swaddling sensation and benefits that the intimate act of love had once reserved for them.

He began to experience withdrawal symptoms of irritability and spike in his mood. Adam struggled to manage his lustful desires, refusing to allow it access and control over him Adam did not want to provoke unnecessary contention and animosity in their home. However, the more he looked on at his partner the more he yearned and lusted after the creature's body and sensual touch. In the arms of his mate Adam found that his worries and troubles would disappear almost instantly during moments of intimacy. Adam had grown dependent on his mate viewing his partner as viable resource and coping tool to distract him from his woes and troubles. Whenever faced with turmoil or adversity Adam turned to his mate to serve as an outlet for him to release and unload his stress and troubles. In his arrogance and temper Adam had unintentionally assigned his mate the role and title of gatekeeper and guardian of his peace and joy. Despite the deprivation Adam found it much easier to manage and carry out his household duties more effectively without the temptation and distraction of lust. Adam held the belief that the act of consummation retained the ability to restore the struggling relationship from its decrepit and worn-out state, however the notion would require compliance and participation from his partner.

Adam often ruminated over the blissful experiences between him and his mate occurring within the confines of the secret garden. The garden of Eden was where the two lovers first discovered the beneficial treasures of intimacy and companionship. The innocent couple would eventually come to explore the physical boundaries and limitations of their anatomies by way of prodding and probing. Adam and his partner furthered the transactional experience assuming a mutual benefits of intimacy and pleasure. The accidental discovery of adulterated delight they soon realized could only be achieved through collaborative cooperation and teamwork.

The discovery of sexual pleasure became a newfound practice and a source of joy for young couple. Adam recalled sentimental moments traveling back and forth through the garden with his mate. He replayed in his mind images of simpler times; days when he and his partner frolicked and played in the myrtle pastures of Eden. His acute imagination recalled all the fondest moments and memories in the garden before their expulsion. The fertile landscape of Eden where the couple thrived was unlike the foreign wasteland they now called their home. The soft cushion of green grass where they once coiled their bodies was now replaced by an empty patch of dirt which provided them little comfort. The gloomy and somewhat terrifying change in scenery did little to help stir feelings of romance and intimacy amongst the couple. The sight of barren landscape produced a defeating sigh of remorse over Adam as he reflected over his past and present circumstances and the outcome of his journey. He attempted to contain his growing frustration accounting the length and duration since he and his mate last prioritized affection and intimacy. Adam looked over at his sleeping companion and began to feel the sensual allure of lust and longing flowing through his body and nerves. Adam found himself studying the contour and frame of his mate's body. His eyes darted back and forth gazing hungrily over his partner like a prowling predator preparing to pounce on its prey.

Adam struggled to maintain his composure all while keeping his lustful desires under control. He attempted to rid himself from the imposition of impure and sinful thoughts however Adam discovered that he was unskilled and outmatched by likes of his own wit and crafty mind. He attempted desperately against his urges but was unable to hold back or restrain himself any longer from pursuing his lustful desire. Adam forfeited the senseless battle seeing no point in depriving himself of the pleasurable experience. Adam's pathology and poor attempt to restrain himself failed miserably. He often contradicted his own logic and justified his irrational behavior with bias reasoning. Adam came to accept that he was incapable of outwitting his growing desire or tame his bulging lust. He dismissed further thoughts on the matter agreeing that the intimate moment had long since been overdue.

Adam leaned inward and began gently rubbing his mates' shoulders initiating the act of courtship. He anticipated that his advances would be fended off and thwarted away, but instead he discovered his caressing touch welcoming. The generous gentle rubs gradually escalated to passionate love making. Their bodies meshed like soft clay just before hardening to form the perfect shape and mold. The sweet, scented fragrance of love and passion lingered and filled the air long after the merriment had commenced. In Adams mind the tense and strained relationship was slowly being mended trailing a reviving path to restoration. The couple agreed to remove defiance and indifference from their partnership, and instead choose collaboration and cooperation. The practice of fostering mutual honor and respect for one another would help to serve and benefit them most. Imparted with a restored sense of safety and assurance Adam's companion now submitted happily to his will. Adam changed his outlook and perspective on his current circumstances and as a result he began to grow more confident in his ability to protect and provide for his family. Adam's advances and other ravenous displays of intimacy were now welcome without reluctance or hesitation. In the eyes of his mate Adam had proven himself worthy repeatedly through his commitment and selfless devotion.

Adam fared well all though he was provided no manual or script to follow as a first-time parent. He was inexperienced lacking in guidance and mentorship. Despite these disparities Adam was committed to upholding the title and role he was assigned to fulfill. He believed like any high bred royal prince facing exile, misfortune and displacement, that his present station was only temporary, and that he would eventually be restored to his rightful place. Adam retained his sense of privilege and entitlement believing rightfully that he was deserving of all the spoils and bounties owed to him by the forsaken and barren world.

10

The Rearing

As time went on, Adam grew comfortable and accepting his assigned role as the head house. He began to settle into his new life growing more comfortable with his designated station in life. Adam coordinated his time setting forth a daily routine and schedule that allowed him to be present to fulfill his domestic obligations. In the morning, midday, and evening times Adam carved out time to be present during those pivotal moments reserved for the nourishment and feeding of their newborn.

Adam demanded to be present during the child's feedings and would often sit beside his partner watching over his mate during feeding. He sat like arbitrator between his partner and child as a precautionary measure prepared to spring into action if needed, Adam was prepared to interject and separate the dominant infant from its mothers' bosoms. Adam stood over the two hovering about like a referee covering an exhibition match. He watched closely over his mate and child eager if not ready to impose his rule. Adam tasked himself with the responsibility of having to detach and separate the fierce competitors.

Adam watched on carefully examining for any trace of abnormalities or signs of distress. He looked helplessly at the hungry child grappling against the weight of bulging bosoms. His sons barbaric and vulgar treatment of the large robust breast made Adam uneasy. The small child glowed radiantly whenever placed near the vicinity of his mother bosoms. The infant's hands clasped securely to the bosoms of its host and drank freely from the bosoms before him. The newborns only struggle was deciding which breast to feast and suckle first. The infant drank greedily from the flowing fountains of rich sweet milk and nectar.

The implementation of supervision was not always a lighthearted, and jovial experience. There were times and instances when Adam was forced to exercise his authority by restraining and pulling the child away from its mothers to keep the small child from devouring and draining his feeble caregiver. Adam preferred the shorter mid-day feedings opposed to that of the longer morning, and evening feedings which called for Adam to be on high alert and extra attentive to the safety and wellness of his mate.

Adam observed how tiresome and fatigued his mate appeared after the completion of each feeding cycle. The act began to induce a sense dizziness over the new parent causing the creature to feel worn down and exhausted. The symptoms of fatigue and exasperation began to set over his mate who could be observed in a deuterating state. A compromising image of his mate slouched over in their child, while in an acute state of consciousness was a disturbing and frightening thought. Adam dreaded the idea of seeing his mate unconscious, with their child left to feast away at the frail body of his mother and host. It pained Adam to watch his son serve as catalyst and tool in the per-ilous demise of his partner and loving companion. The child was a depleting life force devouring the very life and energy from its ailing mother. A feeling of helplessness began to grip Adam along with frus-tration and anxiety. The tensions of guardianship seemed to coil and tighten around Adams nerves and body like harnessed rope.

"Here I stand helpless as a protector" Adam cursed himself, "inca-pable, and battered. It pains me to watch our newborn leeching on its mother like a parasite slowly drawing life away." Adam seemed perplexed beyond the brink of frustration, "I cannot seem to help or aid my mate," declared Adam, "despite brewing and conjuring many recipes and remedies I have only managed to postpone and slow down the deuteriation. I have been unable to concoct a permanent cure and remedy to cure my mate. I have been unsuccessful in delaying the sickness and removing the disease." Adam scolded himself harshly accepting responsibility for the current state and circumstances of his family. Adam blamed himself for the misgivings and misfortunes of which they all endured. The wavering health of his mate's condition was a source of great tension and anxiety for Adam. He was growing more frustrated by the frequency and duration of trails and challenges.

These were truly trying times for Adam who began noticing the quality of his health and wellbeing diminishing. He cried privately many nights outside his home sometimes meters away from his caved den. Adams pride often carried him away from his den treading great lengths the distance before breaking down and imploding. He crumbled beneath the weight of his burdens and troubling thoughts. Adam did not want the sound of his pouring outcries to accidentally fall on the ears and eyes of his beloved mate further dampening the creature's spirit.

"Not even the stars will see my tears", Adam declared, shunning the night sky. He turned his face away from the gazing moon hovering above like a glowing sentinel. The observation of Adams weeping wanderlust was witnessed from aerial view by the watchful moon that seemed to follow and join him on his travels. The experience of weeping wanderlust served as a restorative experience for Adam finding the act somewhat therapeutic at times. His walks became more frequent as Adam was beginning to find joy in the new practice of emotional purification. In was during those walks when Adam would self-examine and attempt to contemplate the interaction between his emotional beliefs and factual truth. The ability to discern between the latter was useful mitigating his strife and grief. In addition, Adam was developing an acute awareness to the benefits of routine sobbing and crying. The tearful act became a practice of distilling sorrow and bitterness through exhaustive refining. The vulnerable moment helped to restore Adam to his senses providing him clarity and moments of lucidity. Beneath the shimmering stars Adam could be seen treading aimlessly without direction, the lit moon reflecting off his back. He paced about the land in deep thought troubled by his burdened spirit.

The stressful position and dual role of being provider and caretaker for his ailing mate and newborn child was a challenging experience. He began to slowly change his demeanor becoming somewhat of a different person. Adam no longer retained his youthful glow becoming somewhat void of personality and enthusiasm. He pitied himself as a condemned figure forced to live a worthless life of servitude. The melancholy feelings which Adam harbored within, did not appear instantaneously or emerge overnight, but rather developed subtly overtime into strong emotions. Adam felt burdened with regret and remorse alongside other troubling symptoms of sorrow and sadness which plagued and haunted his thoughts when reflecting over past times and memories. The slated images in his mind unfurled like budding plants to expose deep seated contention. He stewed more frequently in his attempts to suppress the negative emotions and unwanted feelings brandished deep in his subconscious. The infectious disease of melancholy sadness had claimed yet another victim. The cancerous affliction flourished freely throughout Adam's body contaminating his spirit and overall outlook and perspective on life. Adam carried emotions of resentment deep within his heart which over time began to wither and fester. His famished soul appeared rather dismal, and bleak as if feeding steadily from a despairing regimen and diet of hopelessness.

Adam began to decline in health, his slow deuteration was observable, he fell into a state of deep depression which commandeered his body. The dangerous synergy of anxiety, and stress caused Adams body grow frail and weak susceptible to sickness. Over time Adam began to resemble and look just as ill if not worse than as his counterpart. Stricken with overwhelming fever and exhaustion Adam appeared at times to be disorganized without his wits or senses. He functioned sluggishly moving around his home rambling madly in discourse citing the source of his grief and discontent.

The situation seemed to grow more grave for Adam as he found him-self without appetite for food or basic nourishment. The tension and stress of managing everyday life began to take a morbid toll on Adam's health. His already feeble frame began to show symptoms of exhaustion from lack of nutrition and prolonged absence of sleep. His attempts to obtain rest were at many times foiled by the stringent schedule which called him to remain alert and on-call available at a moment's notice. Adam would not allow himself to fall into a deep state of rest or sleep actively listening out for random sounds or strange noises. The wailing outcries and painful moans produced by his fever-stricken mate denied Adam the luxury and benefit of resting comfortably for long periods. Adam felt as though he was constantly being summoned for the cause and service of caretaking.

One sultry day while out fetching fresh water, Adam caught a glimpse of his himself through the river's reflection. Adam dropped his pale instantly startled by the image looking back at him. He no longer retained the solid tone of his youthful figure or posturing physique. Peering back at him through the still waters stood a shad-owy figure of his former self. The youthful and gentle face Adam once owned was now gone. He could scarcely recognize the lean rugged face gazing back at him from the tepid waters. Adam had become nothing more than a bag of bones in his observation. His worn-down body appearing rather deformed and unshaped could no longer qual-ify him as a youthful specimen. Adam could scarcely stand to look on at his reflection and began to question the state of his very exis-tence. The grave outlook concerning his current path and trajectory evoked a sense of sadness over Adam bringing him to question his life's purpose. His present mind state appeared fixated on self-preser-vation, however unable to produce a permanent resolve to counter-act the aging condition. Adam struggled internally troubled by two opposing forces and ideals. On one end he desired freedom and independence from his responsibilities believing that liberation would alleviate his tension and strife. The latter and less favorable option however constricting allowed him to retain a high sense of pride and honor in keeping his commitment to his family.

Adam once again revisited the thought of absconding to escape the torturous sounds and wails of his child and ailing mate. He held firm to an unshakable conviction and belief that his mate and child were the source of his grief and undoing. Adam fantasized, entertaining for a moment the thought of fleeing and running away; taking with him the little remnants of energy and life that remained. The heralding escape was easily feasible and would have satisfied his deep longing for exoneration. However, whenever faced with the opportunity to flee or run, Adam found that he could not scurry or turn away from his obligations. The arresting weight of responsibility seemed to keep Adams feet firmly grounded. The moral compass that directed his actions would not allow him to desert or leave his family for he knew it was dishonorable and unjust.

Adam was unable to turn away from his family especially in such dire times. "They will surely perish if I leave," Adam argued with himself, "but if I remain living as I do it is without a doubt that I will be doomed as well." Challenged by his innate struggle and internal inclination to life, Adam found himself faced with a precarious enigma of having to choose between self-preservation or the preservation of his family. Adam felt confronted by his own self-interests against the needs of his loved ones. It was easy to understand how feelings of doubt and fear could easily manifest for Adam being placed in such a trying and difficult role and position. There was validity to Adams fears however his distorted sense of reasoning at times caused him great torment and inner conflict. He struggled privately continuously plagued and taunted by a range of uncomfortable and disheartening thoughts. Adam had endured for too the growing pains of adulthood and craved nothing more than to return to the simpler carefree times where he held no commitment or responsibilities.

Adam felt oddly compelled and withdrawn by his reflection and decided it best to return home after a lengthy and most exhausting walk. He arrived home to find the den peacefully silent and serene and walked in carefully stepping delicately with every step. Adam found his usual place beside his mate and attempted to lay down to garner a moment of rest. Unfortunately, the much-needed break was postponed by the sudden outbreak of loud shrieks and cries that filled the air. Adam was tired and physically exhausted; his disoriented and feeble state left him somewhat impaired. He was unable to bring himself up to carry out and fulfill his dutiful role as provider and caretaker. The cries echoed louder carried throughout the cave, Adam could hear the wailing outcry but struggled to distinguish the sound in his weary and tired mind. He did what he could to analyze the frequency and intensity of the noise to determine the urgency and his need to act. Adam listened on closely but still could not discern accurately the sounds that wept, wailed, screeched and shrieked. Adam's tired body was overly exerted and yearned desperately for sleep and rest, he fought hard against the temptation to ignore the call and remain lame in his bed. Adam's heart and wandering mind would not allow him to a rest peacefully until he responded to the noise. Despite feeling overwhelmingly exhausted and deprived of sleep he began to slowly pry open his bloodshot eyes.

Adam awoke to discover his partner missing the creature was nowhere to be found. Fraught with exhaust and concern he began to slowly bring himself up onto his feet, He appeared rather irritated and annoyed for having been disturbed. "I cannot continue to live like this" Adam announced bitterly, "living my days in such strife and misery," He searched the tinted area with tired eyes following the sound of painful moans. Adam mumbled beneath his breathe airing out his frustrations walking through the shadowy cavern. He stumbled over an object on the floor the sudden impact produced a whimpering groan. Adam immediately recognized the strange sound belonging to his mate and partner. The creature did not stir or react from the brushing contact and remained motionlessly asleep in catatonic state weeping and whimpering painfully while still asleep. The odd sighting was strangely bizarre and somewhat alarming for Adam unable to comprehend the strange sounds, and noises escaping the mouth and nostrils of his paralyzed companion.

The squeamish cries appeared rather painful and conjured dreadful images in his mind. Adam's quickly deducted that his partner was experiencing an unpleasant nightmare. One of which entailed some form of abuse, or mistreatment in the dream world. This was Adams only explanation to account for the spell of shrieking screams, and strange jerking motion. Adam was growing rather troubled and uneasy by his partners cries and called out to his mate hoping his voice would awaken the creature from the cerebral trance like state. However, the creature did not stir or awaken exhibiting the strange symptoms of night terror. Adam nudged then shook his mate violently attempting to wake the creature. He was brought to the point of outrage and frustration over the motionless reaction of his befallen companion. "Here lies my beloved mate ill stricken, and near death..." a sudden loud and painful moan escaped the lips of his mate that echoed and filled the room. The piercing outcry triggered Adam's sense of helplessness and fear. It reaffirmed the nagging insecurity and sense of inadequacy he sought desperately to overcome. Having grown quite uncomfortable with the feeling of being useless Adam could scarcely look on at his afflicted companion in such dire conditions.

The hot-tempered feelings of outrage soon simmered transforming itself into sentiments of self-loathing and hopelessness. "I wish I could help you," Adam pleaded kneeling over his mate "but I am helpless to offer you aide. It seems that I cannot save us from this horrid circumstance of our fate." Adams face began to flush, "I have failed to protect you, and our child. And for that, I am a lesser being," Adam eyes began to moisten as he spoke, "How can I be expected protect and provide when armed with honor as my sword, and virtue as my gilded shield. Adam sat beside his partner and gently placed the creatures head over his legs and began combing his fingers through his partner's soft head. "I fear the worst for us, my love," Adam confessed openly, "but we must stay strong and not give in." Adam began to slowly nod off with each passing stroke of his hand. The gentle caress of Adams touch seemed to comfort and sooth his mate bringing an end to the strange noise and jerking motion.

Adam felt weak and fatigued, his entire body was absorbed with exhaustion. The little strength he reserved was now depleted as he attempted to rub away the coals from his tired weary eyes. Adam fought desperately against the urge to fall asleep choosing to abstain from sleep like a tired watch guard. Despite his valiant efforts and pure intentions, Adam was overwhelmed and unqualified to serve as Night's Watch, in his present condition. His tired and overly exhausted body was helpless to fend off the luring siren guiding him to rest and sleep. Adam began to feel to the soothing sense of warmness flowing through his body. He could feel the weight of his eyelids growing dense under the weight of his brows. Adam directed what little strength remained towards his facial muscle in a futile effort to keep from the slumbering state. He managed to raise one brow before finally surrendering his efforts.

Adam was instantly overcome with a sense of calm and serenity. His shoulder dropped suddenly giving him full view his mate and child. His apprehensions, and fears begin to dissipate and fade away disappearing gradually into an irrational abyss of nothingness. Adam was finally at peace, he felt optimistically hopeful that everything would work out for the best. This was Adams first spiritual encounter; he was very much inexperienced in the practice of surrendering his will and relying solely on faith. This moment would forever be engrained in his mind pacifying him as he slept peacefully that night. Adam accepted that the morning sun would soon arrive to cast rays of light and hope, possibly removing the clouds of trouble and misfortune that seemed to follow him and his family around. Adam appeared less resistant to the thought of rest and began to grow more welcoming to the idea of securing a peaceful night of sleep. The revitalizing notion helped to sooth Adams of his worries and ease his troubled mind as he began to prep for rest. He stretched out his arms giving a long-winded yawn, compelled by the sudden call to rest. It wasn't long before Adam found himself laying on the ground beside his sleeping mate and child. The situation was truly a most difficult one for Adam to overcome, however he was unwilling to yield or give up on his family.

11

The Support

One sweltering afternoon when both, his mate and the child were asleep, Adam in his ailing condition set forth under the scolding sun to meet with Tree. He postponed the thought of visiting his loyal friend and overseer for some time. His frantic and somewhat busy schedule did not allow much time for Adam to coordinate earlier visit. However today good fortune presented Adam was with rare opportunity to conduct a hasty trip to see Tree. Adam understood that he had to be quick for there was no telling how long his mate and child would remain asleep before waking up to feed.

With very little time to waste Adam set out on his travels. His eagerness displayed thru his lengthy strides speeding forth to his destination. Adam walked in high spirits his thoughts loaded with hopeful thoughts. "Tree will surely offer a solution to my conflict," thought Adam, "for I am at my wits end." The heat from the sun only helped to encourage Adam to further his speed and pace. "I need more than anything," Adam, pleaded outwardly, "the invaluable wisdom and council of Tree regarding how I should proceed." Adam grounded himself in the reassuring belief that Tree would be able to offer him some form of guidance and assistance to help his ailing partner.

Tree, spotted Adam, from yonder walking towards her direction. His image was spotty, and unclear, and even as he tread closer, she could scarcely recognize her old friend. It was obvious, and visibly plain to see that something was troubling Adam. His body was frail and bruised looking significantly worse since their last meeting. He appeared battered and defeated, thought Tree, observing Adam's thinning demeanor and struggling posture. His bulging eyes, and sunken face filled with anguish was hardly offset by the radiant smile adorned across his face.

Adam was almost unrecognizable his face was bearded and unkempt. His troubling appearance resembled that of a disturbed and ailing individual. Tree was alarmed at seeing Adam in his current state. "It is good to see you," she greeted Adam tenderly, "however, you do not seem like usual yourself, what is the matter?" Adam did not respond however his sullen face and moistened eyes gleaming with dew, had already spoken for him. He behaved rather oddly standing quietly in her shadow. Adam was struggling to overcome the feeling of inadequacy and shame which festered standing before the presence of his loving matriarch.

Adam was not to prepared to disclose his shortcomings or unveil the source of his sorrow and grief. He stood entranced in thought conflicted internally unable to communicate a response. Adam was acutely aware that his strange behavior would expose what he sought desperately to hide. "Are you not well?" Tree asked again, "You seem somewhat bothered and preoccupied," Tree continued prying, "Is everything alright?" Tree waited patiently for Adam to respond before growing worried. "Please answer me Adam for your silence concerns me. Tell me what is wrong?" Tree pleaded anxiously holding back a levy of tears. "Speak to me Adam," Tree implored once again, "you draw no benefit from carrying on in secrecy. Please do not withhold from me?" Adam struggled to lift his head to face Tree, feeling overwhelmed by the estranged feeling the fondness. Adam began to recall the kindling sensation of love and care long since forgotten. The feeling was rewarding to say the most, it felt nice to feel prioritized and regarded with such a high degree of concern and worry.

Tree drew silent, refusing to beg or plead any further. She could hardly stand to look on at him in such a worn and downtrodden state. Adam took little notice of Tree's indignation having yet raised his eyes to meet her very own. Internally Adam struggled with the shameful feeling of unworthiness. He was unable to control the wave of crashing emotions which flooded suddenly . Adam felt once again like a child again standing before his loving matriarch. However, unlike a child Adam resented the fact that he could express his grief and gripes with the unfiltered leverage of prepubescent pride. Adam recalled his many feats and past endeavors remembering the many promises that he made to Tree during the glory of his childhood and youth. Adam was unable to bare the potent fragrance of boyish exuberance lingering through the air. At present the fear of death seemed meaningless to Adam when compared to the thought of disappointing Tree. Adam answered finally with a tremor in his voice and an unshakable sadness in his tone. He began to explain as best as he could the source of his turmoil.

"I do not know where to begin," Adam answered in a barren and humble tone" I set out on a quest to start a family with the most modest and just of intentions. I blindly assumed the role and position of the provider and protecter unwittingly. In doing so I am expected to embark and hold fast to the untamed reigns fatherhood. The burden of responsibility has become an overwhelming task that I have yet to manage successfully." Adam's raised his head slowly to meet Tree's face. The look of embrace was felt the instance the tender two locked eyes. The glaze in Tree's eyes reflected a glossy pane of soft tears which blurred her vision.

"My dear Adam." Tree answered attempting to provide comfort and reassurance. "You have not failed my son." "Yes, I have!" Adam snubbed defiantly, "How can I not feel like a failure, when my family teeters everyday towards the brinks of death and me helpless to provide support and aid to them." Adam began to sob pitifully before Tree "I am most certain that if they fall ill to death, then my end and demise will ensue shortly after. All is doomed for us, if I am unable to find a way," cried Adam, "the very fate of our lives will be sealed soon if no actions are taken." Adam spoke hysterically while flushed with emotions which showed on his face. The tension and overwhelming stress brought the already exhausted and famished body of Adam down on his knees. The very sight of Adams unraveling was nerve wrecking to witness and observe. Tree did not know what to do or how she should respond. She cursed her stoic frame for denying her the ability to reach out and comfort Adam, embracing him tenderly in her arms.

Suddenly without warning a delectable fruit dropped down from above, followed by another. It was not long before Adam found himself being showered by variety of fruits placed before his feet. "Eat," Tree urged, "I beg of you." She offered him nourishment and encouraged him to feed to restore his health. "How can you expect to help your family if you, yourself are not well." She invited Adam to indulge and consume something nutritious to help restore his strength, and energy, however Adam respectfully declined.

Adam was adamant in his refusal and would not accept or eat a single fruit offered. "I am sorry Tree," Adam apologized, "but I cannot enjoy these delicious pleasures while my mate lays ill, and bedridden. And what will come of our child," Adam pleaded swallowing a wad of saliva lodged in his throat, "without his mother how will the newborn feed." He burst into wallowing tears and appeared choked by his words. Adam attempted desperately to convey the sentiments of his greatest fear. He wrestled with his conscious unsure whether he should expel and unpack his troubles. It was obvious to see that Adam was uncomfortable drawing a sense of shame from the fatal possibility and thought. "I... am... Afraid..." Adam struggled to phrase together the words, "that...my mate and child will not survive no more than a few moons."

The moment drew eerie and silent, Tree looked on helplessly as the trail of salty tears poured down Adams grimaced and hardened face. His tears followed a moistened path that led down his rugged face into the patchy course of his jawline. His tears hung suspended beneath the arch or his chin before trickling softly onto the ground and over his feet. Adam was internally conflicted and attempted to thwart away the lingering stench of helplessness that tormented his soul. He appeared vulnerably immature regressing once again to a prepubescent mind set. Adam became awkwardly silent after his admission feeling somewhat embarrassed by the despairing thoughts which clouded his mind.

Highly prideful and critical of himself Adam felt a sense with humiliation at hearing his fears spoken out loud. Adam began to regret the self-loathing pity of his weary outcries. His tears seemed to provoke and punish him incessantly by replaying his admission over in his mind. The distorted recalling was overly dramatized and pitiful than the actual reality. Tree collected her composure and prepared herself to offer Adam counsel. However, suddenly with little warning or provocation Adam began to sob and cry carrying on hysterically. Tree observed that Adam was no longer a child however, his childish behavior resembled that of an obnoxious infant. Adam wailed and carried on like a preschooler with little shame or reservation even folding himself into ball on the ground.

At the very moment Tree was heartbroken, looking on as tears spewed from Adam eyes. The tear ran down and over the ends of his malnourished face. The image of Adam from an outward perspective appeared despairing. The pitiable image evoked that of a helpless child crying out in desperate need of support. It was obvious to see that Adam was at his lowest point. His current state and appearance did not resemble that of a supreme or noble-being. The resilient attributes and dexterity which God, proclaimed and reserved over man was now being brought into question. At present the creature wallowing pitifully on the ground did not seem to be of stable or sound mind. Gauging from his current behavior Adam appeared objectively unfit to carry out the task of caring for a family and home. Tree questioned how well Adam would have fared had he been entrusted with the monumental task of serving as ruler of both heaven and earth.

The term sole heir, and crowned prince were unbefitting titles for Adam who at present took refuge in the practice of self-loathing. Adam wallowed pathetically in a stew of his own pity and self-doubt.

It saddened Tree to see Adam in such a profound and distressing state. Seeped beneath the dirt Tree could taste the whimpers of Adams salty tears absorbed through her roots and vines. Adam sulked miserably with despair dampening the patchy earth. Tree silently analyzed the dire situation assessing rather quickly the severity and seriousness of Adam's current turmoil. She began to formulate a treatment and response to the impeding crises. Tree feared the fatal thought of Adam's death and demise which would mark the tragic end and fall of man.

It was clear to Tree that in the absence of an intervention, Adam and his family would surlily perish. Tree remembered the sworn oath and commitment she made to God offering to protect and watch over Adam. "How can I possibly explain Adams demise and passing to our king?" Tree was burdened with the thought of witnessing God's reaction after being confronted by the egregious news. The foul, and unpleasant thought of God's wrath was enough to provoke Tree to act in support. Deep in her thoughts Tree scoured the trenches of her mind thinking of ways to support Adam during this difficult time. She more than anyone cared deeply for Adam and dreaded the thought of seeing him placed such a challenging and compromising position. She wanted nothing more than to offer Adam relief from his pain and anguish. Wrought with concern Tree contemplated over the matter with intense gravity pondering ways she could of support and assistance.

One might consider Tree's modest call to act as a noble deed that served to benefit Adam's life while simultaneously insuring her very own. "Adam, my child," Tree attempted to reassure him, "I think that I may be able to assist you..." Tree offered her support but stopped immediately after taking notice of the fact that Adam had fallen fast asleep. Tree chose not to wake or disturb the slumbering manchild, and instead chose to let Adam rest. She decided to utilize the intermittent moment to devise a tactical plan of action to provide relief and aide to her dearest Adam.

Adam slept soundly, however much longer than expected. He rested a quarter of the day, approaching the brink of dusk. Adam awoke before the dawning of the orange sun feeling well rested and rejuvenated. He stretched his arms outward and gave a restful yawn before coming to the sudden realization that he was not home. Adam began to panic, "my family," he cried out, remembering that his mate, and child were left unattended. Adam without haste jumped onto his feet and began to brush away the debris and dirt off his body. He started to make his way, but not before gathering a few delectable fruits from the ground. Adam was surprised to discover that the restful experience had helped to restore and return his appetite.

Adam prepared to depart and make his way back home, however Tree stopped him just in time to offer a few soothing words, "Adam, though it pains me to confess that I alone cannot remedy your cause, however return to me on the morrow's night. By then I will have hopefully, conceived a solution and answer to our problem." Adam looked on at Tree baffled and confused by her words. "What are you saying?" Adam questioned, "What is it that you plan to do?" Tree did not respond but instead looked away. "I remind you Tree," Adam urged, "that my family, and livelihood is presently at stake. I need to know exactly what you intend what you to do," pleaded Adam. Tree was reluctant and resisted the temptation to disclose her intentions however it would not be long before she would falter beneath the weight of Adam's snaring glare.

"I will call on your father our merciful lord creator to help aide us," Tree disclosed, "It is obvious that this matter is beyond our control and requires the support and intervention of higher power and force." Adam appeared non receptive finding himself repulsed by the idea of reaching out to his father to ask and request his support. Adam resented the fact that the only person who could help to relieve him of his situation was his absent father. "We must call on God," said Tree, "and pray that the powers of providence and divinity agrees with us." The proposal appeared attractive however unrealistic. Adam was convinced that his creator and master would not agree to aid him, especially not for his sake and mercy of his family.

"Tree, I assure you that my father will not assist us," Adam stated boldly, "have you forget that he is the same vengeful master who banished us from his kingdom. God will not come to save..." Tree stopped Adam before he could finish or complete his thought. "Adam, I have known our lord, and master long before you were created, and though it may seem that he is a vengeful God, he is also kind and forgiving God. "Adam was moved by Tree's testimony. "I will beg and plead for his grace and mercy" said Tree, "and in good faith I believe that God will help us." Before Adam could respond, or offer a rebuttal, Tree dismissed Adam reminding him of his domestic priorities and obligations, "Go on now," Tree implored, "return home to your family, it is apparent that your mate, and child need you by their side more than ever." Adam did not know what else to say other than to offer his gratitude. "Thank you," Adam answered, in a modest and humble tone "for all you have done for me and my family providing us unwavering support." The tender moment was warm and touching, but before the flood of emotional tears could began to set over the pair, Adam decided it best to leave without uttering another word and set forth on the path and direction back home.

12

The Plea

Tree was unable to rest much of the evening, recalling on her encounter with Adam earlier that day. Learning the dire misfortunes of Adam's present circumstances was distressful and kept Tree from securing a peaceful night's rest. Tree was nervous and filled with anxiety about her meeting with the king the next day. She avoided the preemptive urge to predict the outcome of the interaction. Tree felt ghastly mortified considering the possibility that her appeal could be refused by the king. She feared the massive request would be received impartially and bring into question her alliance and loyalty.

Tree could not find peace, nor could she sleep comfortably confined to anxious state entirely void of rest. She sat through the night watching the glowing moon slowly diminishing disappearing gradually into the foreground. Peering up from the horizon was the morning sun arriving just in time to usher in a bright new day. Tree seemed unprovoked by the shifting of the sun standing motionless before the great sphere. Her mind roamed aimlessly arrested by a host of negative thoughts. Tree attempted to detain and gain control of her racing mind through the practice of deep meditation. Tree was preparing her nerves for the critical meeting that would take place. She feared that an inglorious and contentious scene would somehow take play between them. Tree recited different variations and ways to approach the subtle request without raising alarm or suspicion to her merciful plea.

Tree waited patiently watching the busty clouds fade away and disperse allowing for rays of sunshine to bask over the earth. The candescent sphere was now lodged high up in the sky. The peak of the sun's position indicated the opportune moment for Tree to conduct her prayer and outreach to the king. "The time has come," Tree acknowledged feeling a shutter nervousness traveling through her body "The matter is urgent and requires immediate attention," Tree admitted to herself with firm conviction attempting to both convince herself as well as build up the confidence to initiate the sacred prayer, "I must not tarry any longer," She agreed finally, ready to call out to God!"

Taking a moment to gather and compose her thoughts, Tree caught her breath feeling somewhat poised in her preparation to initiate the summoning prayer. She closed her eyes and began to chant the sacred combination of words. In her stillness she could feel the warm rays from the sunlight beaming over her body. Tree sensed the swiftness of the wind ruffling though her leafy green hair. She was attuned with the earth for the most part having been grounded in one accord with nature. Her rooted design enabled for a path and connection that helped to amplify the spiritual calling and prayer. Tree's supernatural abilities allowed her to channel a direct wave and path of communication with her king.

"Our father, our father, our father," Tree repeated softly, drawing in another breath, "my lord, my king, my master..." she chanted on, "God! It is I, your loyal and faithful servant Tree, who calls forth your name," Tree waited for a moment, but noticed nothing besides the wild winds swirling over the dusty earth. She believed that her prayers were being heard, and that God was somehow listening. In those days anyone could outreach and call out to God, but only after reciting the sacred prayer.

Tree was not detoured by the silence that filled the air. She managed to remain neutral to the king's absence accepting the unspoken exchange of pleasantries "I call onto you today my lord," Tree continued "to plead and pray for your favor and guidance." Tree paused with the hope of an ominous interjection, however when none came, she continued again in somewhat of a discouraging tone, "My lord" Tree began her plea, "I come to you today to beg at the mercy of your feet. It is unfortunate that I am faced with an incomparable dilemma that I alone cannot seem to resolve and seek your divine assistance and intervention."

Tree waited for an answer to her plea, but again she received no response. She was beginning to grow rather annoyed by the absence of her king's engagement, and almost hesitated to continue with her request "My king!" Tree furthered, "I am helpless, and find myself riddled with confusion. I know very well that your time is sacred, and that you toil tirelessly in your ordeals. It is not my intent to disturb your practice or peace, however currently I have no other place to turn."

Tree paused again once again awaiting a response but was only met with indignation and awkward silence. Tree became instantly annoyed; frustrated by the kings display of indifference, and quickly forgetting her place and rank began to call out loudly, "God dammit answer me!" Tree flagrantly demanded in an assertive tone "I need your help." It was obvious, to see that Tree was annoyed and was quickly approaching a point of inner conflict. Her tension and frustration began to increase, growing rather upset at feeling unheard and discounted by her king. "My lord..." Tree attempted once again to recite the sacred prayer but was silenced by the booming sound of God's bellowing voice.

"What is it, Tree?" answered God in thundering voice, "Why do you disturb me with your assiduous inquisitions!" Tree, shuddered with fear, her leaves began to tremble as she struggled to answer. Tree stood frozen before the sight of her omnipotent king appearing rather impudent in her thoughts. She was unable produce the correct combination of words necessary to organize a clear and cohesive response. "Why do you berate my name," God sounded angerly, growing rather impatient for Tree to respond. "Speak!" The king commanded" 'you have recited the sacred payer and chosen to interrupt me in the mitts of my affairs. Now speak Tree tell me your reasoning?"

Tree still feeling rattled attempted to regain her composure drawing in a deep long breath. She fumbled through the list of agendas she kept in her mind and scrambled franticly to find an appropriate response to the tempered king. God was growing more impatient, and beckoned Tree to answer as to the purpose and reason for this meeting "Be brisk, and be brief," warned the king in addressing Tree, "You have sung my prayers, and summoned me, yet greet me with silence. I do not understand." God was perplexed by Tree's lack of explanation "Is my time not precious, are my labors not plentiful, so why do you summon me." God's temper was starting to grow increasingly impatient and lacking in temperance.

Tree in her stillness responded with politeness "My king, I do not wish to waste your time," Tree answered apologetically in a respectful manner tone, "I fear the matter is most urgent and needs to be brought to your attention. "Adam your son is ill stricken, and currently plagued with sickness, I fear the worst for his life, and..." But before Tree could complete her thoughts God interrupted, in a firm condemning voice, "Adam, is no longer my son, and frankly, no longer my concern," Tree, was stunned by the rash unexpected response from the noble king, "I am unconcerned with Adam and have since rinsed my hands with man.", "Adam God explained is no longer a boy nor is he an child," God bluntly reminded Tree, "why does he not plead his woes and sorrows before me."

Tree, paused for a moment bewildered by the cruel and harsh behavior of her king. "My lord!" Tree chastised provokingly, "I was not aware that Adam's expulsion from paradise was contingent on his removal from your love and grace." Tree asserted her voice and began to speak boldly to her king,

"I need not remind you, that I was never caste out, nor was I ever expelled from Eden but instead volunteered my services. I made the decision to leave my home in paradise ultimately, accepting my fate without fraught or bitterness. I am only attempting to fulfill and carry out the obligatory duties that you yourself bestowed onto me. So, why do you withhold your support from me as well?" Tree looked squarely into the face of God, and did not flinch or stir in speaking her mind and affirming her truths. Tree eyes were locked on and fixed directly on the king. She held firm to the fidelity of her beliefs refusing to falter or apologize for her crass direct delivery.

"I stand before you today," Tree pleaded, "begging for your continued blessing, and support so that I may continue to fulfill my appointed duties, that is to sustain Adam and keep him alive!" God was electrified by the audacity of Tree's, brazen, and bold reprieve. "How dare you..." erupted the king in a harsh proud voice. The stage was now set for a heated confrontation which would have surely ensued had Tree not interrupted the king offering a passion filled plea. "Please try to understand me God" Tree, cried out, "though you are my king, and creator, master and lord I am truly worthless and without purpose if Adam's life and fate should abruptly come to an end."

Many creatures at the time could attest to God's greatness describing the intensity of his presence as an indescribably illuminating experience. The sheer intensity of God's presence often caused mortals and mammals to look away and shield their eyes. The awkward flute of silence began to fill the air as the two stood gazing back and forth at each other, The dense air felt humid and harsh amidst sweltering tension building between God and Tree. God appeared to be in a state of deep thought and mental deliberation. The standoff which lasted briefly and eventually ended with God breaking the silent tension with an exhausting sigh of defeat. "Alright," God agreed, "I will help you." He gestured with a nod.

Tree was amazed, somewhat astonished by the outcome of her plea. Her words resonated with the shared sense of accountability they both reserved as Adam's creator, and caretaker. The empathetic capability possessed by her king was truly God's greatest quality and served as a testament to his glory and power. The extent of God's kindness and generosity was observed magnanimously through Tree's eyes. She retained a high degree of respect and admiration towards her master and king. Tree was if nothing else, moved by the king's charitable display of grace and generosity. She believed firmly in the eternal bond and solidarity shared between herself and the king. The lasting friendship seemed to precede the likes of time itself. Their spiritual connection was a priceless token like a rare gem or stone unequivocal in grade. The quality of their relationship resembled that of a rare a diamond forged over time through the pressures of extreme conditioning.

Tree saw God through a complex lens of remorse and sympathy. Standing before her was the bruised ego of a father struggling internally to restore his good faith and image. She also saw a stubborn king who was reluctant to confront the veiled truth of his failures or take account his own shortcomings. God was very much still unsettled and filled with disappointments at not being able to complete and carry out his masterful plan. While in the same frame Tree could also see a proud and honorable master emotionally afflicted and torn. In his heart God felt as though the one creature he loved dearly had wronged and wounded him severely. Adam's betrayal had made a lasting impact on the king, the offense lingered over his head like a dark cloud. The unkempt stench of disappointment filled the king with disdain towards his own creation. There was a shift observed in God's behavior as he now appeared reluctant to further his practice of artistry. The traumatic incident had somehow diminished his fiery passion and interest in molding forging new creatures. God was still annoyed if not irritated by the consequential outcome and turnout of his most recent attempt. It was easy to see that God did not want anything to do with the rebellious man creature, however, he could not shake away the burden of responsibility that weighed over his mind and heart.

Tree advanced on speaking with wholehearted sincerity, "I left your side only for the sake of duty and nothing more. Why should I too, be subject to your neglect?" God raised his head to look up Tree, "Your highness please excuse my forwardness, but I simply refuse to be absent from your love or removed from your good grace." God paused for a moment cradled by his thoughts, he gazed on silently at Tree as if beginning to slowly recall how generously thoughtful and, affirming Tree was in her nature and design. God recalled another instance when Tree was just a budding stem enriched with great potential, she was gifted with ability to permeate an entire garden. Tree was co-founder and part creator of Eden, the beautiful paradise of which she had committed most of her existence and energy. She assisted the king by ensuring the welfare and stock of his many creations. Tree was appointed with the responsibility of maintaining an entire colony of God's creation and creatures which she rightfully assumed despite never having been granted or afforded the luxury of freedom and free will.

God was skeptical of the Tree's intentions as she stood before him pleading for the welfare and life of another. It appeared that Tree's questionable loyalty to her master was now compromised leaning favorably in the direction of Adam over himself. Surprisingly, God was not upset or surprised by the change in their dynamics. He observed that Tree had gained a cohesive bond with Adam having been formed through decades of rearing. Trees presence and efforts seemed unfairly matched to God in his remote and extended absence. God could only listen on to his old friend with estranged regard, however her appeal brought a soft look of worry over the king's face that resonated with the thoughts and emotions he felt but was unable to share. God was moved by Trees appeal regarding the matter, her views though subjective demonstrated the organic a love of a parent advocating for their child needs. Tree's intentions were pure, and innocent as observed through the windows of her masters' eyes. "Hmm." God moaned agreeably, "I see now that you right."

Tree was pleased by God's sudden reception and acknowledgment. She felt a sense of relief in her king's reprieve however curious as to what sparked the sudden change of heart. Tree did not dismiss the effectiveness of her appeal but was still uncertain as to the impact of her defense in helping to sway the king's decision to support Adam. "Something does not feel right," Tree thought herself seeming unconvinced and somewhat questionable as the motives of her illustrious king. She decided it was best not to disclose her suspicions and avoid stirring up tension in a moment that called for celebration. Tree silently waited to hear the king's next words with the growing hope that his commands would dispel and put to rest any suspicion or doubts regarding the intent of her master.

"I suppose that you are right Tree," God admitted openly, his words rung triumphantly like music to her ears. "You have never caused me grief, or allowed for ill will to stir between us. You have proved yourself to a noble creature pure in heart and gentle in spirit. Your intentions are modest, and often draped in generosity and kindness for others. As a token of gratitude for your service and lifetime commitment I will offer you my assistance and support in good faith." Tree could not help but feel moved by Gods affirmation and was finally receiving the recognition she had desperately sought. Tree rejoiced cheerfully and quickly dismissed her prior suspicions having been convinced of her king innocence. Tree listened attentively at her lordship words not daring to interrupt.

"Upon your branches" God continued, "will grow a special fruit a potent and ripened apple. This special apple when ingested will cure Adam and remove from him any sickness or ailments that troubling him. Adam will be restored back to good health." Tree began to feel a tingling sensation taking place within her body. The strange sensation soon began to intensify, growing somewhat uncomfortable. Tree soon found herself overcome with pain but refused cry out. She understood the toll of her request would entail a large and hefty sum however, Tree was unprepared to pay the taxing price. The unbearable pain forced Tree to cry out no longer able to hold back her tears. Suddenly right before her eyes an apple began to form appearing on a single branch. The bright golden apple which appeared ripened to perfection was low a hanging fruit positioned for easy retrieval.

"Give Adam, the apple," God encouraged, "a single bite will be enough to make him well again." "Thank you, your gracefulness," Tree repeated crying out joyfully, "providence is truly your name." God declined Trees compliment stating that her gratitude was unnecessary. "The merit of honor belongs to you my dear friend, for your unwavering commitment in fostering and caring for man." God's recognition, and acknowledgment was a warming sensation that could turn around and rejuvenate the most downtrodden and lowly of creatures. "Sadly," announced God, "I must now depart and take leave. Goodbye for now Tree but believe I will be seeing you again very soon my faithful friend." And just as God appeared from subtle nothingness, so was his departure and disappearance into thin air. Tree once again found herself alone marinating in deep thought. Tree recalled the entire incident replaying it over in her mind. She struggled to recover from the excruciating pain endured, somewhat uncertain and questionable to the process the events that had just taken place.

13

The Intervention Pt.1

The day came when Adam would return to meet with Tree as instructed. He set forth on his voyage curious to the outcome of Trees meeting and interaction with God. In his mind he imagined the many outcomes, and scenarios that played out all leading to the same outcome, and conclusion. Adam was not entirely optimistic and held firm to the small grain of hope that the turnout and meeting with God was successful, and that Tree was going to deliver good news to help relieve him of his current troubles.

Adam traveled the usual path to meet with Tree. The lengthy distance never seemed problematic however due to Adams feeble condition the trip took longer than expected. Adam arrived at Tree's post and received a grand reception. Tree was in the most pleasant and gayest of moods, already in a celebratory state, Tree could hardly contain her excitement. "Come Adam," she encouraged him to come closer, "I have quite the tale to share." Adam did as he was told and took his usual place at her side. Tree began to share and retell the intimate engagement with their king. At the end of the telling Tree presented Adam with the golden apple from her branch. Tree struggled to recall the exact words of her king and attempted to recite and rephrase the simple prescription. "A few bites," Tree recalled, "should bring you back to your healthy self again." Adam was elated by the good news and struggled to hold back his excitement and joy.

"Thank you, Tree," he cried out, I am most blessed to have you as my nurturing guardian, and dearest friend."

Adam was granted permission to retrieve the apple and hoisted himself up high to grab the tasty fruit from Tree's branching arm. Adam did not plan to disclose or share out loud his secret plan. He had no intention of eating the apple alone, but instead planned to share the delectable fruit with his ailing mate. Adam held the apple tightly in his hands and began to examine the fruit looking closely over the shimmering apple that seem to shine radiantly beneath the glowing sun. Adam stood entranced gazing at the apple with growing fascination and interest. He appeared fixated over the delectable fruit.

Adam was lost in his head, venturing the uncharted wilderness of his own thoughts. In the face of the sun, the shiny coated apple was a relishing sight. Adam ruminated for a moment on the severity of his situation and considered the dire details or his current circumstances. The thought of having obtained a cure for his ailments brought a smile over Adams face. His sense of humor drew laughter viewing the irony of his current predicament. Adam perceived his troubles and worries as monumental, and overwhelming however in the eyes of God, his worldly affairs, and problems were viewed as minor and trivial. God resembled an expert physician skillfully prescribing small doses of medication to his over exaggerative and ailing patients.

Tree took notice to the fact that Adam had not bitten or attempted to taste the delicious fruit. She saw this and grew somewhat alarmed by Adam hesitation. She offered encouragement, "Adam the sooner you eat the sooner you shall regain your strength, and energy." Adam could hear Tree however his attention was very much fixed on the golden apple before him. Trees voice faded in and out echoing in the background, but Adam could not make out her words.

He appeared withdrawn very much consumed by his imagination. Adam entertained the endless miracles and possibilities that could be afforded as result of the golden apple. He relished over how much simpler his life would be after his mate was well again. "Can this apple," thought Adam, "really help to restore and cure my mate, removing the plaguing sickness that torments my beloved..." "Adam!" Tree called out in a loud and stern tone. The sound of her voice shook Adam and caused him to fumble over the golden apple. The fierce call was enough to startle any creature and worked effectively to stir Adam from his lucid daydream. "You should eat the apple now," Tree encouraged, "so that you may regain your health, and energy to care for your mate, and child Ka..." Tree found herself struggling to recall the name of the newborn child's and fumbled embarrassingly to remember the infant's name.

"Cain," Adam interrupted, "my son's name is Cain," slowly, peeling his eyes away from the apple, turning his attention back over to Tree, "You are absolutely right Tree," Adam agreed, "I must not tarry any longer, and should not waste time eating the apple here." He explained, "Instead I will enjoy the apple on my homeward bound travels." Adam gathered himself hastily, and speaking rather quickly he offered passive assurances. "Tree if this apple works as well as you described, then I shall arrive home fully restored in peak physical form...." Tree did not get a chance to speak out or offer a response or rebuttal "Thank you again," Adam cried out embracing Tree with a warm and gracious hug. "I will be back to visit you soon," He promised excusing himself somewhat rushing off quickly in the direction and path from he came.

Tree was uneasy, and felt a bit disturbed by Adam's brief encounter, and although she usually took Adams words at face value, she could not escape the strange and eerie feeling that fell over her. She could not express fully the daunting feeling of remorse that haunted her. The nagging suspicion of deception resembled that of her interaction with God. Tree could not explain the unwelcoming emotion that seemed to gnaw and eat away at her from within like a virus infecting her mind with senseless ideas and notions. The nagging suspicion irritated her mind beyond the point of ease. She found herself drawn and somewhat consumed by the overwhelming question, "Why would Adam, want to deceive me?" Tree stood for some time thinking and pondering attempting to deduce between reason and logic. Growing tiresome in her endless pursuit Tree was unable to produce substantial motives to pin and keep in place her nagging suspicions.

With out much evidence to support her unfounded accusations, Tree once again dismissed her suspicions as baseless and unwarranted. "Preposterous," Tree thwarted the vulgar thought, "I will not stain Adams good name with impure and senseless accusations. Adam is honorable and full of virtue fully embodying the maleficence of his creator. He serves as direct reflection of God's honesty and generosity. Adam is the living embodiment of all that is sound and good in this world." The affirming reminder of Adam's benevolence helped to smother the cautionary flames that burned deep within Tree's conscious.

Undoubtedly compromised and blinded by her affection and love for Adam, Tree actively chose to ignore and dismiss her inner skepticism. She believed that disclosing her personal inklings would only help to garner friction between the two. Tree decided it best to absorb the positive moment and to refocus her energy on the spoils of her victory. She decided to savor and enjoy her triumphant win rather than challenging it. Tree was left feeling good for having obtained the respect and honor of her devoted king, right along with the winning favor and admiration of her beloved Adam. Tree stood firm and proud rejoiced with fulfillment at the fact she was able to offer Adam assistance and helped him to avoid a tragic end.

To Be Continued....